Frances Freeling Broderip

My Grandmother's Budget

SALZWASSER
VERLAG

Frances Freeling Broderip

My Grandmother's Budget

Reprint of the original, first published in 1863.

1st Edition 2022 | ISBN: 978-3-37500-125-4

Verlag (Publisher): Salzwasser Verlag GmbH, Zeilweg 44, 60439 Frankfurt, Deutschland
Vertretungsberechtigt (Authorized to represent): E. Roepke, Zeilweg 44, 60439 Frankfurt, Deutschland
Druck (Print): Books on Demand GmbH, In de Tarpen 42, 22848 Norderstedt, Deutschland

MY GRANDMOTHER'S BUDGET

OF

STORIES AND SONGS,

BY

FRANCES FREELING BRODERIP;

WITH ILLUSTRATIONS BY HER BROTHER,

THOMAS HOOD.

LONDON

MDCCCLXIII.

JENNY WREN'S CHOICE.

Page 42.

CONTENTS.

MY GRANDMOTHER.

MY GRANDMOTHER was the dearest old creature that ever lived in the world,—and it was a sad, sad day for us, children as we were, when she went out of it to a better land. Now we all had happy homes, and the best and kindest of fathers and mothers,—who loved and cared for us more than many fashionable fathers and mothers do for their young ones now-a-days. For instance, we always breakfasted, dined, and drank tea with them; for it was the creed in our family, that, as we hoped all to spend many years together, the best way to spend them happily was to begin early in the way we meant to go,—so there was no banishment to kitchen or nursery for us. Those of us, whose parents were not rich in "world's gear," were told they ought to be all the better off in other things that lay within their own power,—so that, looking back after the lapse of many years, I can remember the least prosperous of us were the more carefully trained at home in the little refinements of manner, that are not above or below *any* rank of life. And the wholesome seed so carefully planted in the virgin soil by sensible fathers and loving mothers, has grown, blossomed, and borne fruit, in one or two lives, that were so humbly useful and truly good, they were not valued till they were lost to this world.

> "So angels walked unknown on earth,
> But, when they flew, were recognized."

And of these beloved parents we cannot think now without grateful tears of love for their memory.

But our Grandmother was another kind of being altogether. She had long passed the battle of life, in which our dear ones were striving and fighting so gallantly. She was a noble veteran, whose scars bore witness to many a hard-fought field; but she was set aside now in dignified retirement to rest on her laurels, — and to encourage those still in the ranks, — as well as the little cadets, who had not yet smelt powder. She was a grand-looking old lady, too, with a handsome Roman nose, and decided profile — softened and cheered by eyes that were still bright, and that could twinkle like a child's at any fit of merriment. Ever since we could remember her, she used to be dressed in a dark maroon-coloured merino that fell in soft full folds round her still upright figure. No dingy blacks for her, to look dismal, ("and dirty, my dear!") but rich dark reds like the colour of very old port wine. A clear starched handkerchief was pinned daintily across, and kept close at the throat by an antique brooch, described formerly as a "cat's eye, set round with markisites." I despair of describing her cap, for it was unlike anything I have seen since, not aspiring to the height and dignity of a turban, but far transcending all ordinary caps, and made of the richest point-lace. The dear old soul used to be very particular over her attire even then, and she used to say to Barbara, her staid waiting woman :—

"I know I am an old woman, Barbara, and some folks think I ought not to waste time in such things; but I don't see why, because people are aged, they need be ugly. I can see that the Almighty sends as fair green leaves to aged trees, and as sweet fragrant blossoms to old bushes, as he does to young ones; and I should like my dear children and grand-children to have a pleasant memory of me, when I shall have laid my earthly garments away."

So, whenever we went to see her, there she was, neat and shining like a new pin, and as merry as a cricket. "I like fun, my dear, as well as ever I did," said she to a somewhat demure young matron; "and as for my grand-children, they get lessons at school and training at home, as they ought; so I like them to have nothing but enjoyment when they come to see their old granny. To my notion, there's too much knowledge now-a-days stuffed into young heads; and I think they get so grey all the quicker for it. In my young days, when we worked, we worked; when we learned, we learned; and when we played, we played. There was no jumbling up of arithmetic and dolls, or grammar and goodies, then. We learnt our lessons, and had our play afterwards; and I do think, what we did learn, was thoroughly taught and well mastered, though there was no royal road to learning with short cuts. And then we had real fairy tales—the White Cat and Cinderella, and Blue-beard. People can't write such things now-a-days without turning the giants into steam-engines, and explaining all the wonders, as Mr. What 's-his-name does his chemical experiments at the Polytechnic. Indeed, my dear, the fact is, that children are now all so fearfully clever, their elders must be half afraid to speak to them; and the old vulgar proverb, to have anything in it, ought now to be revised as:—'Teach your grand-child how to suck eggs!'"

She practised her own theory, too; and one of our chief delights in paying her a visit, was to hear her old-world tales and ballads. For she used to croon in the sweetest, trembling, pipe in the world, snatches of songs and ballads, like an aged blackbird. Those were such days to be sure!—not too often; and therefore the more eagerly longed for. We used to be dressed in bib and tucker certainly; but not in things too fine for mortals' daily wear, for she would not tolerate stiff collars and tight frocks in her house. First, we had sponge cake, and tiny wine glasses of old currant wine, so clear and syruppy, that we all had an indistinct tradition it was brewed for Cock Robin's nuptials. Then, if we were very good, we saw her make the pie with her own hands; for that was one of the institutions of the house. The snowy cloth was spread, and the equally white paste-board and tapering ebony rolling-pin set forth in the daintiest order. I never taste cherry-pie now without a lump in my throat at the recollection. Ah, but they don't know how to make pies now —that art died with my Grandmother. Never since has been made such melting flaky crust, disdaining all soda, lemon, or other mean puff-raising inventions—never such just proportion of fruit and sugar, such a delicious mingling of the whole. The delicate china cup put in for the juice, the graceful cutter that shaped such *fleurs de lys*, and roses for the edge, they are all lost to posterity with the hands that used them. When she rolled up her clear muslin apron for the last time, and sent it down with the paste-board and rolling-pin, science lost a great light, and, with the last corner of the last of her pies, those delicious dainties became extinct.

Then, when that solemn operation was over, and every sign of it carefully removed, she sat installed in the corner of the sofa, in all the dignity of black silk mittens and brilliant, and emerald hoop rings, and beguiled the time while that ambrosial pie was acquiring a delicate hue in the oven, by tale and song. Many of them are as lost to us as the departed generations of pies, but some few have been saved from the ravages of time, and these are offered to the young readers of the present day, in the hope that they may, at any rate, take some little interest in this feeble shadow of the dear old lady who lives in our fond memories as "My Grandmother."

THE PEDLAR OF STILDORF.

STILDORF lies in a retired nook at the foot of a vast mountain, nestled into it like a wallflower in the crevice of an old stone, or a swallow's nest in a hole under the eaves. Thick woods of dark pines clothe the steep sides of the mountain to its summit, save here and there, where laborious toil has succeeded in clearing a space and planting a vineyard. The village, niched irregularly up and down as the need or fancy of the builder devised, overlooks a plateau of land, mapped out into rich corn-fields or luxuriant pastures sloping downwards, through which winds, with a stately curve, the arrowy rushing river, bearing on its broad breast many a heavy-laden barge, or picturesque raft of floating logs.

It is a secluded little spot, for the simple skill

and industry of its inhabitants suffice to supply its humble wants and frugal fare, and it has no intercourse with the world beyond (shut in as it is by mountains on the one hand and the river on the other), save when its great market, held once in three years, brings strangers to supply its few luxuries, by bartering them for the native produce. Then Goodwife Bertha exchanges the work of her busy wheel and thrifty fingers for the gay-coloured stuff for her Sunday gown, or the smart kerchief of many hues; while her rosy-cheeked daughter, Scilla, obtains the long-coveted necklace of Venice beads, or tucker of Flanders lace, in lieu of her carefully hoarded store of yellow cheese, and tubs of salted butter. The holland for Master Pieter's holiday shirt is chosen, after a world of haggling and rubbing, by his keen spouse, and the price of it, as well as that of the choice tobacco equally carefully selected by himself, is deducted from the value of the pipes of wine he brings to the market. Good racy wine is it too; and it will glide down the throats of many a lace-ruffled, dainty connoisseur, who does not care to know that it is the blood of the generous fruit, which hung on the vines of the mountain-side some glowing summers back, and which has since then seethed, bubbled and matured in his great cool cellar.

What a holiday is this great fair to all the dwellers in Stildorf! Months beforehand, preparations are diligently made for it, in great brewings of sour hard beer; and for weeks previously, the housewives are busily kneading, rolling, and baking, cakes and pies; while the children, like practised skirmishers, make vigorous and unexpected descents on currants, almonds, and sugar. Days before, young fir-trees are planted in the green-turfed square before the church, and booths erected to hold the glorious wares that are even now on their way, in packs and panniers, on mules and asses, through lonely passes and steep roads, over the great mountains that separate Stildorf from the rest of the civilized world. The day before the fair is formally opened, gardens and hedge-rows are stripped of their blooming treasures, for garlands and decorations; and strings of flags of every imaginable hue are suspended across the few streets, wherever it is possible (which is somewhat seldom,) to get houses to match in aspect and height. Then, when fleecy clouds are streaked with the pale rosy early messengers of the sun—the heralds clad in crimson and gold whom he sends to prepare his way—all the youthful population of Stildorf is awake!

Fat feet are hastily thrust, wrong side before, into holiday blue stockings and silver buckled shoes, and Sunday-going scarlet hooded cloaks huddled over chubby little neck sand shoulders, while numberless shocks of cropped, plaited, and curled hair, are twisted and arranged in unwontedly speedy fashion by their owners. Many a careful mother scolds over the untasted milk, and untouched barley cakes; but who cares for breakfast or scolding, when the fair, in all its glories, lies stretched before them! Such lanes of booths, such ecstatic trumpets and drums, such magical shows and entertainments

—such square feet and yards of gingerbread, hundredweights of candy, and legions of dolls and whistles! The children of Stildorf, in their secret hearts, unfeignedly believe that Fairyland is only a perpetual series of fairs, and human bliss *can* go no further!

But all pleasures below the moon must come to an end, even fairs, and the usual chartered fortnight had expired; for Stildorf people have a larger appetite for merry-making than some other folks we know of, who have had enough of their saturnalias in three days at farthest. The Stildorfers, like the rest of their nation, are a calm phlegmatic race, who no more dream of hurrying over their pastimes than they do over their meals, and, therefore, deliberately set to work in a systematic manner at both, and waste no crumbs of either by the way. Still, I repeat, even the course of a Stildorf repast, pickled apples, boiled goose, roasted calf's head, eel broth, cherry tart, cutlets in raspberry sauce, and carp stewed with plums, becoming exhausted in succession, must find a termination at last; and so likewise the fair came to an end.

Of the radiant glories of its pristine brilliancy, there only remained bare planks, withered garlands, trodden sawdust, and greasy paper; among which relics of the past the children wandered mournful and spiritless, like young Romans haunting the ruins of the temple of Jupiter Tonans.

In the small market-place, the principal spot and centre of the fair (for it branched in various channels, in narrow rows of booths up steep streets, and canvas pavilions in unexpected corners), in the market-place, I say, stood the hostel of the place, (for Stildorf boasted of but one,) from whence the short-kilted maid of the burgomaster fetched his worship's jug of local double X, and where the choice spirits of the place assembled in the evening, to play ninepins, and imbibe potations only christened with that single initial. Linden trees sheltered the front of the house, from one of which hung, on a projecting branch, the sign which proclaimed entertainment for travellers, whereon the native artist had exhausted his skill in depicting a white hart with a golden crown between its branching antlers.

On the day after the fair had ended, three comrades, kindred spirits, were sitting in the parlour of the little hostel, discussing some choice "strong waters," in their ancient quaintly-shaped glasses, and canvassing at leisure the proceedings of the past fair. A most engrossing topic, to judge by the eager way the three heads were laid together over the little round table, and the three noses met in earnest argument. While they were thus settling the affairs of nations, and the Stildorf world in very particular, a pedlar entered the room, and laying aside a heavy pack he carried on his shoulders, he sat down at a table close by.

It was not usually the Stildorf habit to address strangers first, partly because few such articles came in their way. However, fair-time opens most people's hearts; and so Master Dort, the miller, a fat contented man, whose broad jovial smile would have propitiated a stock-fish, took upon him the first word.

"Good evening, friend! How have you fared in the market? 'Tis to be hoped you carry back an empty pack and a heavy purse."

"He's a fool if he answer that question, or owns to either case," remarked Grüm, the smith, a big burly man, whose swarthy complexion and dingy garb, as well as his harsh gruff voice, which sounded like a grating rusty hinge, suited his occupation well enough.

"I have no reason to complain of my luck," answered the pedlar quietly, "and as I never carry my gains with me, I have no need to fear owning it!"

"Ah! I suppose you are one of the lucky ones of the world!" said Max, the weaver, with a deep sigh. Now Max was a great contrast to both his companions; for he was a tall gaunt man, with a discontented stoop in his shoulders, caused by his work at the loom; and his lank hair clung straight down by the side of a thin unhappy face, lighted by a pair of lack-lustre eyes. His arms and legs were as attenuated as his own empty spindles, and his voice was compounded of a whine, a drawl, and a snuffle.

"I have had my share as well as others," answered the pedlar drily, as he sat down to his supper, and gravely proceeded to discuss it. He was a spare little man, with not an ounce of superfluous flesh on his bones, or a scrap of unnecessary ornament about him. He had short hair, and but little of it; and his clothes fitted as if they grew on him, skin-fashion;—while the most remarkable things about him were his eyes,—large, dark, and penetrating; they seemed to read the very secrets of the heart.

Then to the aforesaid company came in two more guests: the first, Father Dik, the cobbler of the village, came for his modest pint of sour Stildorf beer, and screw of tobacco,—his fair-time indulgencies,—for he was a very poor man and had no money to spare for luxuries. Hunger was the sauce he mostly had with his dry bread, and incessant toil softened his hard bed of straw for him.

After him came hopping and skipping, full of antic and grimace, Master Spitz, the tailor, who was always shocking the prejudices of the staid folks of Stildorf by his wild ways, which of course at fair-time were generally aggravated, but at that period also more tolerated, owing to the universal licence of the time.

"Hey day! what 's up now?" cried Master Spitz. "Whom have we here? A pedlar with his pack, by all that 's wonderful! Open your goods, my friend, and exhibit. May be, you 'll get a customer here to clear off the fag-end of your wares!"

"I 've shut up shop for the day," answered the pedlar, placidly continuing his supper.

"You 're not up to your trade, if you throw away a chance customer," laughed the jolly miller, taking a huge pull at his tankard.

Then they all laughed, and Spitz, the tailor, and Dort, the miller, so beset the pedlar, that he got up from his half-finished supper and spread

THE PEDLAR OF STILDORF SHOWING HIS WARES.

Page 18.

open his pack. And now he shook off his taciturn manner, and began to expatiate pedlar-fashion in praise of his goods.

"Here," said he, unfolding a short wide cloak made of some shining white material, "is a useful article for a man to pass through life with. It will wear all his days, as long as he requires it, and keep him from harm at the last."

"I wouldn't wear such an old-fashioned thing!" said Spitz, the tailor, twisting round the garment between his finger and thumb, and turning up his professional nose in high disdain at it.

"I don't want white clothes," chuckled the miller, to whom the pedlar offered the cloak, "my wheel paints me white enough for nothing!"

Then the pedlar exhibited a pair of stout shoes, but the upper leathers were very thick, and the soles were of wood, so that they appeared somewhat clumsy, and Max, the weaver, to whom the pedlar offered them, exclaimed :—

"I don't wear clogs, master pedlar, I could not work my loom with such hoofs as these!"

"They are so big, I could take a walk inside them!" grinned the monkeyfied tailor.

"You seem hard to please, master," said the pedlar, turning sharp on him; "but I've something that ought to suit you: here 's a hat that will more than repay its owner for wearing it!"

"You don't call that thing a hat?" growled the surly smith, derisively. "It 's a saucepan without handle or lid!"

"I vow I wouldn't be seen in it if you would give it me!" lisped the tailor affectedly.

The pedlar smiled, and replaced the rejected articles; but, feeling deep down in his pack, he brought out a short straight staff, which he put into the smith's hand.

"I don't want walking sticks," snarled Grüm. "I could cut a better any day in the nearest hedge. Look at this straight thing with never a bend or a knot in it from end to end. I'll have none of it!"

"You don't seem to speak *your* opinion,"

said the pedlar to Father Dik, who had been quietly looking on, but saying nothing; "don't you think any of these articles would find a purchaser in *you*?"

"I should like any of them, master," replied Father Dik; "but the fact is, I'm a very poor man, and work hard and live from hand to mouth, and so have no money to spare for such things."

"You seem a quiet civil sort of fellow," said the pedlar. "I've something here that would be of great service to you!"

"It's no use," replied Father Dik, shaking his head. "I can't pay for it."

"Then I'll tell you what I'll do," said the pedlar, "I'll trust you till you can. See here," and taking out a large curious-looking pair of spectacles, he fitted them carefully on Father Dik's nose, "if these suit your sight, and you would like to have them, I'll leave them with you till I come again, which won't be yet awhile."

Old Father Dik, in great delight, stuck up

his head and peered proudly about with his spectacles.

"St. Crispin defend us!" cried he. "I can see better than I could when I was young. But it 's no use, master, you 're very kind; but I never had a debt in my life, and I 'm too old to begin now, so take them back again, with many thanks for your offer."

"You seem a very upright kind of man," said the pedlar, approvingly, "but we won't fall out in the bargain. I 'll leave them just for trial for a few weeks, on the sole condition that you never take them off, except when you go to sleep."

Old Father Dik scratched his head, and looked at the ceiling and pondered over it, and, at last, overcome by the temptation, agreed to the pedlar's offer, appointing to pay him so much at a time, and by way of the first instalment foregoing his customary beer and tobacco. Off he hobbled in great glee with his prize, vowing in his inmost heart to work double tides till he got the whole sum to make them lawfully his own. Then the pedlar packed up his wares, settled his reckoning, and departed in the twilight, no one knew whither.

When he was gone, Spitz and Dort began to repent that they had not become purchasers too. "I might have got that cloak very cheap by beating him down a little, and it could have been altered to a better shape," muttered Dort.

"I almost wish I had looked closer at that hat," observed Spitz.

"I might have saved the shoes for wet days after all," grumbled Max; "but it's just my luck."

And the neighbours, like all people, who too late begin to covet things they refused when within their reach, departed to their several homes in no pleasant mood.

After a while, as a stream subsides into its glassy quietness again, when the stone that invaded it has sunk, and the ring-ripples grow larger, and finally disappear, Stildorf resumed its usual state of placid vegetation. Labour went on as usual from dawn until sunset, and people ate, drank, and slept as usual; while the very children played their accustomed games at the street-corners, as if no such important event as the fair had broken in upon their tranquil life and humdrum amusements. But as years rolled on, a change came over several of our acquaintance, and, in more cases than one, not for the better.

For instance, Max, the weaver, who had been always known to be a discontented idle fellow, who would never work till he was obliged to do so, and who laid the blame of all his misfortunes on his evil luck, grew worse and worse. So that, at last, the busy house-wives, finding that it was in vain to wait till he chose to weave the fruits of their thrifty spinning into linen and woollen stuffs, took the unprecedented step of inviting a strange weaver to the village, and patronizing him in a body. So at last Max's loom always stood unfed; and he fell into utter poverty, till he came merely to exist on chance charity for a meal.

"Ah," muttered Father Dik with a sigh, "poor foolish fellow, he would have made his fortune, if he had taken the pedlar's goods into wear; for the Shoes of Perseverance would have kept him fast to his work."

Grüm, the smith, got into a sad scrape, too, for he was heavily fined for swearing that he had put four new shoes on the worshipful the Burgomaster's mule; when it was proved in open court that he had only filed the old ones, thereby endangering the safety of Stildorf's chief magistrate.

"The straight Staff of Truth would have steered him out of that mischief; while falsehood has brought its usual punishment," observed Father Dik to his wife.

Spitz, the little tailor, offended all his customers so with his foolish remarks, that he, also, lost the best part of his trade. When he proclaimed the fact that the Burgomaster had a hump on his back, and proved that one of the priest's legs was longer than the other, he offended these dignitaries mortally. And they had been his chief customers; but from henceforth they took the trouble of going once a year to Oberstein, and getting fitted with new garments by more judicious Snips; and all the little stars of the place followed the example of these big comets. So that Spitz had only the fag-end of his old custom, and obtained merely alterations to do for poor old tattered garments, or orders for new suits from customers who did not pay.

"If he had put Tact on his head with the pedlar's hat," quoth Father Dik to himself, "he would be still the chief tailor in Stildorf."

But the worst misfortune of all was Dort, the miller's, who on one snowy night was caught in the Burgomaster's yard at unlawful hours, having been courting his worship's daughter, and drinking his worship's beer. He had hoped to escape notice by hiding behind the great rosemary bush; but his dark wooing garb, donned for the occasion, was so conspicuous against the white snow, that he was found out, and then and there suffered summary punishment at the hands of the enraged functionary, and this in such an ignominious manner, that he did not show his face again at the White Hart for full twelve calendar months after.

"The white Cloak of Innocence would have been mighty useful to him after all, poor man!" said Father Dik.

As for Father Dik himself, he lived soberly and honestly as before, and still, by the aid of his spectacles, looking always at the bright side of all things. So that to his mind, his low thatched hovel seemed a very palace, his coarse fare, a comfortable banquet, and his old wife, the comeliest and sweetest woman in all Stildorf. Morning, noon, and night, he sat cheerfully at his work and whistled his merry tune. The pedlar never again made his appearance in Stildorf, though eagerly watched for by Father Dik, who,—in dire distress what to do with the money he owed him, carefully and faithfully hoarded, through many a sore trial of privation,—at last by the advice of the priest gave it to the poor.

"How is it, Father Dik," people would say

to him, "how is it that you are so cheerful and easily satisfied; you are as happy as a king!"

"Because," said Father Dik, "I wear the spectacles of Content, through which a wise man looks upon the world!"

THE LITTLE QUEEN.

TO-MORROW is Amy's birthday,—
Amy, our pride and our treasure;
What can we plan, and do for her
To give her a little pleasure?
We will gather under her window
So early in the dawning,
And sing a merry birth-day song
To wake her in the morning.

We'll raise a throne in the meadow,
We'll make it of moss and heather,
And gather the brookside rushes green
To bind it well together.
We'll weave her a flowery garland,
Befitting her royal station,
A bulrush tall shall her sceptre be
At her solemn coronation.

The bees shall bring their honey,
  A convolvolus bell for chalice;
The greenwood for a spacious hall,
  And a bower for a palace.
Her subjects shall gather round her,
  Before her footstool bowing,
By hill and lea, by blossom and tree,
  Their faithful service vowing.

Throned in her innocent beauty,
  Her sweetness a royal vesture,
She will move us all to obey her
  By every gentle gesture.
Sweet temper is her dower;
  All hearts to her service moving,
The reason we choose her for our Queen
  Is because she is so loving.

For Alice is tall and stately,
  Her ringlets are dark and flowing,
And Mary carries a merry sound
  Where'er she may be going.

Isabel's fair and slender,
  And Helen is bright and pretty,
And everyone crowds round merry Maud,
  Because she is so witty.

But our own dear little Amy,
  Amy with soft brown tresses,
No one remembers how she looks,
  No one thinks of her dresses.
She is always sweet and winning,
  Tender, serene and steady,
No wonder she wears the lily crown,
  For she is our Queen already!

A GAME AT CARDS.

"I SHALL give a party!" said the Card-Table. "I have just been newly French-polished, and I know I look exceedingly well; moreover I have just had some beautiful green cloth put on, so that I am quite in apple-pie order! I shall give a party: I have made up my mind to it."

"I can't think how you can be so foolish," grumbled the Card-Basket, "at your time of life you ought to know better, and it will be so very unpleasant for me to look for lodgings elsewhere."

"Why we shall all be obliged to move, then," chattered the china ornaments, "what a nuisance to be sure. There is one thing certain, the Card-Table will remain vacant to the end of the season; for when we have found comfortable new abodes at Mantelpiece-place or Chiffonier-crescent, it is not to be supposed we shall unsettle ourselves again, just to fill his empty room!"

"I don't care," persisted the Card-Table, who had become ambitious after his renovation, "If I remain empty for the rest of my life for it, I will have a little gaiety for once; and so I shall give a party, and ask all the Cards in the pack!"

"Oh goodness!" lisped the Scent-bottle, "how vewy vulgaw! Why evewybody knows cawds are quite gone out of fashion. Any one *distingué* has acted chawades, or pwovewbs, or definitions at least. It is only the scwubs who descend to cawds now!"

However, the Card-table had made up his mind, and was not to be persuaded out of it, so he sent separate and special invitations to the sixteen Court Cards, who formed the aristocracy, and a general circular to the rest of the pack, who were nobodies.

It ought to be remarked, as an unprecedented circumstance in the history of parties, that all those who were invited came; but it should be understood that, as a rule, Cards are a very clannish set of people, and never part company except for Ecarté or Piquet, when all ranking below a seven are excluded. On this occasion, however, they all came in their glory, for they were a new set of people, who possessed clean faces and brocaded backs, so that they were not to be lightly esteemed.

The evening came, and all was prepared in readiness; a couple of pure wax candles, in silver sconces, being placed on the board of green cloth. The company arrived, and were ushered to their places; and now began the trouble of the unfortunate party-giver, for everybody quarrelled for precedence in the most disagreeable manner in the world.

First of all, the Kings and Queens fell out with the Aces as to who should have the first places; and the royalties got the worst of it, for the Aces proved their claims, as allowed by Commerce, Whist, Piquet, Loo, Speculation, and Pope Joan, whilst the Kings and Queens could only bring Ecarté, Cribbage and Quadrille on their side. So the Aces took the highest place in great glory, while the Knave of Clubs laughed slily, and whispered the Nine of Diamonds, who was called Pope Joan, that he thought he should try for the first place himself.

"How absolute the Knave is!" laughed the bed-post Four of Clubs.

"Quite right, too, to stand up for our privileges," said the Knave of Spades; "don't we count one for our nob, and two for our heels?"

Matters, however, were not coming to a settlement yet, for the Aces having gained the first place, quarrelled among themselves on whom it should devolve. The Ace of Clubs urged precedence as Basto; but the Ace of Spades overruled him, and the other two Aces as well, by enforcing his rank as Spadille and also because he alone, of all the company, paid rates and taxes! So he was put at the head of the company. Then the Card-table began to arrange a little amusement, and proposed several sorts of games. The King of Clubs suggested playing at "Old Bachelor," but he was voted ungallant by all the suit of Hearts in a body. So they fell to general conversation, and Great Cass condescendingly asked Little Cass how he fared; while Pope Joan and Pam made themselves generally agreeable. The Kings and Queens were, taken as a whole, rather a dull exposition of matrimony, till the Knaves stepped in and made it a little more amusing.

Then up got the Seven of Clubs, and offered to teach them a new game called "Which"; but though the King of Spades, the Queen of Hearts, and the Knave of Diamonds seconded him in the most gallant way, the rest were all so stupid, he was obliged to give it up in despair. Then the Card-table in the hope of making his party go off well, set them playing the game of the Four Trades. But that did not answer at all, for the King of Spades did not like to be named "Spade, the Gardener," the Knave of Clubs would not own "Club, the Constable," as his father; the Queen of Diamonds would not be called the wife of a glazier, and the King and Queen of Hearts utterly scouted the notion of a butcher's trade; while the Nines and Tens made such mistakes as to who were "wigs" and who were "walking-sticks," that they ended in utter confusion all round.

And then the little folks, aping their betters, began to give themselves airs also. The black Deuces and red Sevens disputed who should be "Manille," and the red Nines snubbed the poor Seven of Clubs in the most heartless manner, because he was a new comer, "*which* was not well known!" Then the Card-table, in desperation, set them all to build houses, which answered exceedingly well, and diverted their attention; and they had even reached four stories high, when the Seven of Spades, in his rage that the Nine of Diamonds should be placed over his head, twitted him, and called him the "Curse of Scotland!" And thereon a battle royal arose among them all. The Kings took the head of the field in opposition to the Aces, having the Knaves as their seconds in command. But the Queens basely deserted their sovereign lords and seceded to the Aces; while the mob of Common Cards went on this side or that as they liked. And so they played "Beggar my Neighbour" till they were almost black in the face, the Card-table looking on, and consoling himself with the idea that fighting was nearly as good as feasting; and at any rate it kept things going.

In one corner, a desperate single combat went on between the King and Knave of Hearts, who had long been at secret enmity, on account of some stolen pastry, prepared by the fair hands of the Queen of Hearts herself. Long did the battle rage with varying success, till at last the King of Hearts, uplifting his mighty club, brought the Knave down on his knee, and being then and there vanquished and sorely punished, he vowed repentance and restitution; whereon the gallant King raised him and forgave him, and the fair Queen bestowed on him the flower in her hand as a token of friendship.

When they joined the rest of the party, they found them all making pancakes, and trying who should spring highest; and this served for the supper being laid out in grand style on the cloth. After supper, as is usual on such occasions, they waxed very merry; and some one even went so far as to propose a little fortune-telling; but this so horrified the rest, that they declared the wine had got up into his head, and with one consent they made a pool of "Fright!"

And now the old clock in the corner, in a brief and witty sentence composed of twelve emphatic words, told them that it was time for all respectable folks to break up and go to bed. And, to tell the truth, the Card-table was very glad to hear of it, for he was not used to giving parties; and he had discovered it was more troublesome, and not half so pleasant, as he had imagined. But, of course, you know, he could not say so; and, therefore, he politely pressed them all to remain, and vowed he was grieved to part with them, while in reality he had hardly a leg to stand on, he was so tired, and his valves shook and creaked as if they had the ague.

And then the Ace of Spades, as in "duty bound," returned a vote of thanks from all the company for an agreeable evening; and they set off on their way home. I am sorry to have to relate, that the Knave of Clubs picked all the Kings' pockets; the King of Hearts eloped with the Queen of Diamonds, and the Queen of Hearts was escorted home by the other three Knaves in a body. The worst of it all was, that Pope Joan and "Which" went prying about after everybody; and next day sent a full and detailed account of it all, to each of the daily newspapers, so that the scandal was something prodigious. And the poor Card-table was so ill and upset at the whole affair, that he lost two of his castors, and went lame ever after. And the consequence was, that his old lodgers jeered him in the most unmerciful manner whenever they met him.

"How did your party go off?" called out the Card-basket, who now resided at "Centre-table Hall."

"I heard, but I don't believe it for a moment," remarked the Scent-bottle, "that your fwiends all had too much pancake for supper!"

"How many stories did your house get to?" inquired all the China Ornaments, of Chiffonier-crescent.

But the spirit of the Card-table was extinct; he had burnt out his candles, and he never gave any more parties!

LORD WAGTAIL'S WOOING.

FAIR Jenny Wren sat in her bower of leaves,
And warbled a lay calm and clear,
Lord Willy Wagtail came and sat on a rail
And whispered sweet words in her ear.
"Oh Jenny!" says he, "pray listen to me,
"I love you as none loved before,
"Of this poor little heart, there is not a part
"That throbs not for you evermore!"
But Jenny she curtsied, and blushing rose-red,
Thus unto her wooer said she,
"That love is the strongest, and lasts the longest,
"Which mates with its own degree!"

Lord Wagtail cried out, "My faith do you doubt
"So firmly devoted to you?
"The fond turtle-dove shall be false to his love,
"E'er I will prove ever untrue:
"And, dearest," says he, "I cannot agree
"To any such fanciful thing,
"For a bird that's so fair, with qualities rare,
"Is a suitable match for a king!"
But Jenny still smiled and answered him thus,—
"My Robin 's the bird for me,—
"That love is the strongest, and lasts the longest,
"Which mates with its own degree!"

Lord Wagtail says he, "What! Robin?" quoth he,
"A clown in a flaring red vest,—
"With never a groat, and a russet-brown coat,
"Who lives in a shabby old nest!
"Your beauty and grace, the charms of your face
"A station of rank would adorn;
"A carriage and four, and guineas in store,
"Are the honours to which you were born,

"Sweet Jenny!" he cries—but Jenny replies
With an anger that 's pretty to see,—
"That love is the strongest, and lasts the longest,
"Which mates with its own degree!

"'Neath my Robin's red vest, beats a true tender breast,
"That never knew wrong or deceit;
"And love without cease, contentment and peace,
"Can make any humble lot sweet.
"Your carriage and four, and guineas in store
"Can't save me from all ache and smart;
"Jewels may shine, and gay broidery twine,
"Above a most sorrowful heart.
"So the humble red vest, the lowly thatched nest,
"And my own faithful Robin for me,—
"For that love is the strongest, and lasts the longest,
"Which mates with its own degree."

TIDDY'S TRANSGRESSIONS.

"TIDDY! it is you again! I can't turn my back for a moment, but you must get into some scrape. There, and there, and there, you naughty child!"

Pussy was in a mighty rage with her kitten; for she had been called away from a delicious dinner of cold fish bones to settle a clamorous dispute among the small party in her basket. Tiddy was the youngest and least of the family, and was pushed about and ill treated accordingly, Spot, the eldest, was a tortoise-shell, mottled with black and brown in the most charming manner; in fact she had been pronounced a beauty from the very first, and gave herself airs in consequence. Minnie, the next, was black, and so fat she was like a little ball of sable fur, and was rolled about and admired immensely; while Snap, the next, was no beauty, having a tabby complexion; but was gifted with such strength of will and person combined, that it made up for his want of personal charms. But poor Tiddy! she was small, thin, and weak; and moreover ought to have been white; but, like all young animals of very fair complexion, her earliest days were only remarkable for a general dinginess. Pussy was very fond of all her family, but she had been hitherto celebrated for remarkably fine children, and Tiddy's smallness, —and there,—it must come out! *skinniness* of aspect seemed a sort of disgrace to the comely middle-aged matronly cat.

"You should be more active, Tiddy," said she. "I'm a great deal older than you, and yet see how much I get through in a day, and have all my family cares besides. You don't eat half enough to keep your bones covered, child; you ought to take a walk before breakfast of a morning, to give you an appetite."

Tiddy could have observed it was unnecessary;

for that she was generally hungry enough, the real difficulty being in getting food. For when the saucer of bread and milk was put down by cook in the morning, Spot engrossed the front row, Minnie put both feet in it, and Snap got off with all the big bits, so that what with pushing and poking, Tiddy's share was but small. But to hear the list of Tiddy's misdemeanours, you would have thought she was as fat and strong as Minnie, and as long-limbed and active as Snap. The glass fish-globe was thrown down one day and broken, that somebody might feast on the unfortunate gold fish it contained; and universal consent named Tiddy as the culprit, although as Spot was not so hungry as usual that day at dinner, suspicion ought to have fastened on her. Then a whole pan of cream was lapped up in the dairy which Tiddy likewise bore the blame of, though Minnie's fat sides most likely benefited by it. When the pane of glass in the larder window was broken, Tiddy was in hopes she would be acquitted, as her short legs and little strength could scarcely have achieved the mischief. "You little sinner, you know it was you," growled Snap, "and you picked the cold chicken, too, and ate the whole half pound of butter!" added he, licking his lips.

"I might as well be a thief at once," sighed Tiddy, "as be accused innocently like this. How much injustice there is in the world."

"Oh, Tiddy, Tiddy!" groaned Pussy, as she came in after a fatiguing day's work among the rats in the barn. "You 're the one trouble of my life, and I don't know what I shall do with you. I have only just entered the house, and the cook says you have broken a sauce tureen, and two wine glasses, besides a bottle of wine, which you must have drunk dry first! I never heard of cats drinking wine in my time; but really you do such extraordinary things, Tiddy, that I am not surprised at anything I hear of you. However cook's hunting for you to drown you, she says, so if you take my advice you 'll keep out of her way for a while!"

And Tiddy, in great bitterness of heart,

determined to take the advice to the letter, and French leave, too; accordingly she set off to find a fresh home in the world, hoping the blame of other folk's sins would not follow her there. Many months after, her mother, now occupied with another promising brood of young kittens, received a visit from an elegant stranger. Her coat was as white as snow, and her fur was as soft and sleek as the finest white satin; while round her neck was a superb scarlet morocco collar, with a fine buckle that shone like gold.

"Good evening, madam," said Pussy, curtseying low to her visitor, and pushing aside her young kittens rather unceremoniously in order to offer her a seat.

"Your name is Pussy, I believe," remarked the elegant stranger, "and you have a daughter named Spot?"

"I had," replied Tabby, with a deep sigh; "but she was so handsome, and had such rich fur, we believe some cruel wretch stole her for the sake of her skin; for she disappeared one evening, and has never been seen since."

"Really," observed the fair white cat, "that is sad, indeed; but she was not your only child?"

"Oh, dear, no!" answered Pussy. "Minnie, my next out of that brood, was as fine, fat a kitten as you would see on a summer's day. But she was drowned, poor thing, by accident; while she was helping herself to some milk, the shelf gave way and she fell into the wash tub. And Snap, her brother, was shot by the keeper for killing some young pheasants. Indeed, I was very unlucky with that family!" sighed Pussy.

"May I ask what became of the youngest, Tiny, or some such name?" said the white cat, gravely.

"What Tiddy?" said Pussy, staring with amazement. "Poor Tiddy; she was a good little thing after all, and I am afraid bore more blame than was her share. She ran away: but I should like to know what became of her."

"I can tell you," answered the strange visitor; "she happened fortunately to take the road towards the parsonage, and Miss Rosa, the vicar's daughter, chancing to notice the poor forlorn little thing, kindly took her in. In that house she has been protected and fed with the kindest care. At first, what with being gently spoken to, and escaping from cuffs and kicks, she hardly knew herself. Then when she was fed on good plentiful, wholesome food, and had a warm bed to lie on, she very thankfully answered to her new name of Mite. With all her former troubles, the very name of Tiddy has ceased to belong to her, and nothing but praises of Mite's merry ways, and Mite's charms, are to be heard at the parsonage. I dare say now," continued the snowy creature, rising up proudly and stretching herself to her full height with a graceful wave of her tail, "I dare say, in the well-fed, well-grown cat before you, it is almost impossible for you to recognise the little dirty neglected kitten. However, mother, I am not very unforgiving, and I am quite willing to say no more of the past; now that Mite's magnificence, has blotted out the memory of Tiddy's trials and transgressions!"

ONE STRAW.

A TALL spike of Wheat grew in a large corn-field. In sowing the wheat, some of the seed had been dropped carelessly here and there, so that it grew up out of the ordinary line of the regular furrows. The grain from which our friend sprung had fallen by the side, so that he grew by himself in the midst of a blooming tuft of wild flowers, who were more kindly disposed to receive him, than he was to acknowledge them. The poppies patted him on the back, in the most amicable way possible, but he called them "flaunting things," and would not speak to them. The bindweed twisted her graceful green wreaths round him, and caressed him

THE OLD TOAD AND THE WHEAT-EAR.

Page 52.

gently; but he cast her off roughly, and told her to be off, for she was a "twining sycophant."

So, one by one, he utterly offended, and shut out the gentle denizens of the wheat-field; and they held aloof from him, and left a bare circle round him, in the midst of which he stood up stiff and proud, like a yellow spear.

"How can you be so thoroughly unamiable?" asked an old Toad, who was resting himself under a large cool dock-leaf hard by, "what makes you snub all your friends in that uncouth fashion? Are you ill, or out of sorts,—unwell, or out of temper? Has the sun scorched you up too much, or the rain forgotten you?"

"No," replied the Spike of Wheat, sulkily, "none of this has happened to me; but I am unhappy, discontented, miserable!"

"Then you are greatly to be pitied," answered the old Toad gravely, "for those folks who are well fed and clothed and have great advantages, and yet are unhappy, are the most hopelessly wretched creatures in the world, for they make their own sorrows."

"I am not unreasonable," grumbled the Wheat-ear, "but just look at me; what am I fit for, and what will be my fate? I should like to be a bright member of society—to do great things—and have my name well known in the world. And I am a mere straw! only a straw!"

"And yet you have a great work before you," said the Toad, "come, I am older than you are, and have seen more of the world; now, shall I tell you what your fate will be, as well as those of your brothers?"

"No, thank you," said the Wheat-ear, haughtily; "I don't approve of fortune-telling."

Then the poor old Toad, so ungraciously repulsed, went away and talked to the Poppies, who were very glad to see him, and invited him to supper, for he was an old friend of theirs. Presently a little boy and girl came through the field, and they had a bunch of wheat-ears in their hands. Our friend drew himself up, as straight and stiff as he could, hoping that they would select him to add to their bundle; nor was he disappointed.

"Here's a famous tall fellow here, Lucy!" said the boy, "we must cut him very carefully."

"Be sure you cut off his head without shaking out the corns," answered Lucy, "for the wheat-ears are all so very ripe now, Harry, and my pigeons will have such a feast!"

"It was very kind of Farmer Stokes to let us pick these odd ears by the way," said Harry, "but then he knew he might trust us, and be sure that we should only gather the stray ones."

While the little ones chattered, they gathered the Wheat-ear, and tied him and the rest of his companions in a neat bundle, by means of a green rush. Then they carried it carefully home, when Harry cut the straws in nice pieces about a foot long, and gave the tops to Lucy for her pigeons. Evening came, and when it was nearly dark, Harry and Lucy were perched up at table by their Papa's side, while he taught them how to play the game of "spillikins," with the help of the straws and a little hooked stick. The children were delighted. Lucy laughed so that she shook the straws, and could not mark one for her pains; while Harry stuck his elbows firmly on the table, crossed his legs, bit his lips, frowned, and drew a long breath, and a straw from the heap. Presently, he was so successful that he had a little pile of straws he had taken off without shaking the others. Then Lucy, in her excitement, knocked his elbow, and away they all went on the carpet. She was very sorry for the misfortune, and picked them all up but our unlucky friend of the corn-field, who had tumbled under the leg of the table, out of sight.

"I am one short," said Harry, "I know I had nine, and here are only eight!"

"Never mind," cried Lucy, eagerly, "take another out, it is only a straw. We can get plenty more to-morrow. What does it signify? Why make a fuss about a straw!"

Our poor friend lay miserable and flat under the table. "It's what I always knew," said he, "What does it matter? Its only a straw!"

"Only a straw, Lucy!" replied her Papa; "only a straw, and what then? Suppose you were building your house, and were just one brick short—only a brick—and yet your mansion would not be complete without it?"

"Only we don't build houses with straws, Papa!" said Lucy, rather pertly.

"Perhaps, not; but the birds do, Miss Ignorrance," replied Papa, "and even we human beings, if we don't build the walls with straw, are glad to make use of it for the roofs. Thatched roofs are shady and pleasant as well as pretty, and keep out the heat of the summer sun, as well as the cold of winter frosts, more effectually than slates or tiles."

"But they are getting old-fashioned, Papa," said Lucy; "people don't use thatched houses now: even the cottages are tiled!"

"More's the pity, my dear, I think," observed her Mamma, who had been listening to the conversation, "and perhaps one reason why they are not so common now, is because straw is getting too scarce."

Our friend under the table pricked up his ears at this, as things seemed taking a more favourable turn for himself and his family.

"Yes," continued Papa, "I dare say you would laugh at me if I tell you that your 'Jack Straws' are members of a wide-spread family, that have employed the population of whole villages and factories!"

"What do you mean, Papa?" asked Harry, "what other use is straw put to, besides thatch and bedding for cattle?"

"It serves as bedding for man, too, my boy," answered his father, "witness the straw bed of the poor homeless beggar, in some barn or out-house!"

"And indeed, Harry, it serves richer folks as well," said Mamma, "for most people use straw mattresses under their wool and feather beds!"

"Then," said Lucy, eagerly, "It makes bee-hives—pretty round bee-hives, and the comfortable chairs and stools named after them; like yours, Mamma!"

Our friend the Straw felt quite charmed at the vision of the glories of his race opening before him, and he managed to edge out one end, so that Harry espied him, and picked him up.

"I've a little more respect for you, my friend," said Harry; "but, Papa, what do you mean about whole villages and factories."

"Ask Mamma, there," answered their Father, "how she saw our friends made use of in our Suffolk home!"

Mamma readily responded to the appeal, and described how the straw was cleaned, bleached, flattened, and cut in little machines, and then plaited in long pieces, which were afterwards sewn together and formed into hats and bonnets. She told them how she had seen little children standing at the cottage doors, and plaiting away in the quickest manner possible, almost without the necessity of looking at their work, so expert were they. And then Papa narrated a visit he had paid to a large manufactory where they made straw into paper.

"Indeed, Harry," said his Papa, "I think that is really the most important use that straw is put to now-a-days. The little common wheat-ears, as they grow in the fields among poppies and corn-flowers, little dream of what their future destiny is to be, and that after a while they will be made into nice paper, upon which letters may be written that will travel to all quarters of the globe; or on which, as newspapers, the intelligence of great towns will be printed, to travel perhaps through the length and breadth of the land!"

Who now so proud as our friend the Straw: he swelled with importance, and stuck up more stiffly than ever.

"I, too," he cried, "may perhaps be one of of these wonderful messengers of good. I, even I, may form a part of some message that will thrill the heart of a great empire, and rouse to life a whole people!"

But our friend, having been permitted to see far off the glories of his race, was not destined to realise in his own person such an exalted mission. Harry and Lucy played spillikins with him till they were tired of the game, and then Mamma took possession of him and his brothers, and made use of them for her gauffering-board. And finally, Papa coming home very warm and tired, wanted some sherry cobbler, and took the straw to drink it with; so that our friend enjoyed the privilege of tasting real wine with sugar and ice in it.

And this was the last sensation he was fated to experience, for having been left in the glass, he was carried down into the kitchen, and thrown on the fire with some other rubbish.

"What a disagreeable smell of something burning there is, Mary," said Mrs. Smith.

"Please, ma'am, it's only some old straws I threw on the fire," replied the cook. And so this was the end of one straw.

SAND MASONS.

I'M going to build a castle,
So stately and so tall,
With loophole, tower and battlement,
And many a rampart wall.
I'll dig a moat around it,
And throw a bridge across,
'Twill stand a twelvemonth's sieging,
Defying storm and loss!"
Uprose the gallant castle,
Fit to o'erlook a fray,
But the waves came creeping up it,
And washed it quite away.
Down came tower and battlement,
Down went bridge and wall,
The victor sea swept over it,
Came up, and conquered all!

"I'll build a goodly oven,
  And wall it up in sand,
And it shall furnish bread enough
  To victual all the land.
The loaves shall bake on this side,
  The rolls be ranged on that,
A stone shall make a goodly door
  To close it firm and flat."
The oven it was built up strong,
  And filled with loaves of bread;
But creeping came the hungry waves,
  And ate them up instead!
Away the loaves went floating,
  Went cakes and rolls away
The greedy waves had, sure enough,
  A goodly feast that day!

"I'll lay me out a garden
  And build a shady bower,
I'll plant there dulse and tangle,
  And many a shore-grown flower.

Stone-crop, and yellow poppy
  That by the ocean dwells,
Shall grow there, and the border
  Be purple mussel shells!"
The garden throve and prospered,
  One whole long summer day,
But the tide came up at evening
  And washed it all away.
Far borne upon the surges,
  Did weed and blossom float,
And every purple mussel shell
  Was turned into a boat!

" I've made a lofty island,
  Its sides are firm and steep,
And it rises like a rock-bound land.
  From the bosom of the deep."
Then the angry waves came roaring,
  With hoarse incessant din,
Broke in spray across the island,
  And led their forces in.

It smaller grew and smaller,
  As the billows travelled on,
Till one huge wave rolled victorious,
  And the little isle was gone.
There are plenty of older children,
  Who their sand foundations lay,
But the tide of life sweeps o'er them too,
  And washes them all away.

THE RAIN AND THE WIND.

THE Wind and the Rain met one day: "Hail, fellow! well met!" said the Wind, with a friendly puff.

"I greet you heartily," murmured the Rain; "where do you come from?"

"Many places," answered the Wind. "I am sorry to say, I was not in a very good temper yesterday, and so, as a matter of course, I did a great deal of mischief."

"Well, I did not feel amiable, myself, the other day," said the Rain, confidentially, "The fact is, there was something amiss with the Clouds; the Sun and they could not agree; he wanted to shine, and they were in a hurry to send me down to the earth: so we all had a regular quarrel for a while. However, we don't fall out long, so we made it up, and hung out the rainbow flag of peace. Then I was suffered to go on my way; but I confess I was not in an amiable mood; I vented my cross temper on the earth, and poured a perfect deluge upon it. I got in at the holes in the roofs of the houses, and damaged the furniture inside. I swelled the rivers and canals till they overflowed the wheat-fields and drowned the cattle. I soaked the hay that was cut in the meadows, till it was good for nothing, and saturated the corn till it grew green and sodden. I even washed the very fruit off the trees, and knocked and battered the flowers to pieces, so that the damp earth was covered with the many-coloured petals. Indeed, I am heartily sorry now for my gust of temper, for I am sure I must have done a great deal of harm."

"That's but slight mischief compared with mine," replied the Wind, "for I went to the sea, and I raised such a tempest that it was strewed with wrecks and spars, all over. Then the Lightning and his son, the Thunder, would interfere, and add their part, to make matters worse, and between us all it was a very awful scene. The waves rolled mountains high, and black as ink, with great dark abysses between them, that seemed enough to swallow up any ship; and the blue forked lightning flared on the white crests of the waves, while the thunder made such a noise, that even my voice was not heard. I expect that gale will be long remembered along the coasts, by the merchants and shipowners who have lost their gold and their vessels, and the widows and orphans who have been deprived of their bread-winners. But I am sorry now for what I have done!"

"Then let us mend our ways, brother," said the Rain, "we will do all that can be done by those, who have committed wrong; we will repent and do better. Suppose you and I set forth on our travels now, and see how much good we can do to make up for the past."

"Agreed," cried the wind, with a hearty puff; "we will set off at once, and meet, this evening, by the sea, when the tide comes in, and tell what our doings have been."

Now the Rain had a very easy task for it, for since his last misdeeds, the Sun had come out, like a warm-hearted luminary as he is, and had done his best to repair the mischief, but he had almost overdone the matter, for he smiled so brightly and blazed so fiercely, that everything was almost dried up. Then the rain came down gently, very gently, and refreshed the parched earth; and the green trees waved rejoicingly, and the corn was thankful for the shower. The little flowers lifted up their heads, and smiled again with their innocent eyes; while the brooks and streams flashed back rejoicing glances from their silvery faces. He laid the dust in the roads, so that the tired wayfarers on foot, and the gaily-dressed folks in carriages, all cried out, "How pleasant the rain is; and how sweet everything smells after a shower!" He washed the inky roofs and dirty pavements in close cities, and swept away a great deal of unwholesome rubbish, and the poor, thin, overworked toilers looked up through the dim windows of their workshops, and thought how the grass must be springing, and the daisies growing, in the green fields far away. Then the Rain went steadily on with his work,—raining on the rich and the poor, the good and the evil, sending wholesome draughts alike to pleasant and shady gardens by the river side, and to dingy courts and alleys, with stunted trees and parched turf; for it is only man, who makes distinctions, and not God's servant, Nature.

"Mother, mother," shouted little Mary, "your water-butt is brimming over, we shall be able to have such a wash! Baby shall have clean pinafores every day for a week!"

Then the busy mother ran rejoicing out, even with cracked pans and leaky tubs, to catch all she could of the precious fluid.

"Only think," said the Rain, "how some people want what others waste. Of all things in the world, fresh air and clean water ought to be among the things folks have plenty of."

It would take a long time to tell all the good deeds the rain did; how he filled the ponds and set the water-wheels going; how he freshened the grass, and cleaned the windows, and made himself generally useful and agreeable; but we have not much time, and must not forget to see what the Wind was about. First of all, he went round to the flowers, and apologised for his rough behaviour, like a gentleman as he was. He kissed the rose so softly, that she unfolded her leaves, and gave him an odorous sigh, as a sign of her forgiveness. Then he frolicked with the acacia blossoms, till they laughed so, that they fell off the tree.

"If you really repent of your evil deeds," said the Rose, "and wish to do all the good you can, my sisters and I will give you an errand of charity. In yonder window sits a poor little crippled child, whose weak limbs are nevertheless hastening fast to the better land. We have all tried to reach him, but the window is too high; but you can get there if you choose, and bear our perfume on your wings."

The Wind joyfully consented, and the Roses, Pinks, Honeysuckles, Mignonette, and all the sweet flowers that grew on the spot, loaded him with their balmy breath to carry to the sick child. And the Wind held them very tight, and blew in at the tall window, and breathed them all in a delicious breath round the child's face. Then the Wind fanned his faint brow, and kissed his weary eyes till he smiled, and said the angels were nearer than he had thought. When the wind came down again, the daisies and pansies called out to him:—

"Dear Wind, blow a little stronger! We have no sweet scents to send him, but if you will lend us a strong puff, we can give you some of our pretty coloured petals!"

The Wind very gladly consented, and again went on his kind errand. Then he laid a purple pansy leaf and a white cistus flower in the boy's wan hand. And a smile came again on the pale lips: "I wonder if there are flowers in heaven?" said he. "I hope there will be daisies there too!"

Then the wind being of a restless nature could not long tarry there; so off he went again, and set the sails of the mill going. Round and round they went, like the wings of huge birds, and round and round went the great stones, grinding the ripe yellow wheat into snowy flour for the children's bread. "'Tis an ill wind that blows no one good," chuckled the dusty miller, as he stood by the door; and his little fat daughter sang, in her merry voice:—

"Blow wind, blow, and go mill, go,
That the miller may grind his corn,
That the baker may take it, and into rolls make it,
And bring us some hot in the morn!"

Then away went the Wind again, over hill and moorland, ruffling the feathers on little downy chickens, and setting the "tottering grass" shaking as if with fifty agues. He did no mischief certainly; but he could not resist a few bits of fun. For instance, he blew Dame Trot's cap up into a fir tree, so that she was obliged to call John, with his ladder, to get it down; and he distributed the washing she had hung out to dry differently to what she had done, by sticking a shirt in a furze bush, and taking one stocking north into a pond, and another south to a hay stack, and sending all the other pairs setting and shuffling as if they were out at a ball. He took Tommy Todd's kite so far out of sight that the child danced in terror, thinking he should never see it again, when, rush, flap down it came at his feet. Then the Wind carried off the reverend Doctor Short's shovel-hat, and popped it safe down on a hive of bees. Out came the little workers in a mighty fuss to know what the black thing was; and Roger was obliged to get a washing-prop and remove it from a respectful distance, while the poor doctor was broiling in the sun with a pocket-handkerchief over his bald pate.

Then the Wind spread his wings and sailed far away till he came to the great Sea, which now lay calm and smooth beneath him. So he rippled the little waves, and sent them far up on the hard-ribbed sand, and played with them till they grew quite merry, and glittered and twinkled in the sunbeams like silver. The Wind fluttered the wings of the great seagulls;

and puffed up their feathers till they were quite huffy with him for taking such liberties with them, but he did not care for all their airs, for he had plenty of his own; so he laughed at them and then went on his way. And he came to a fair stately vessel that lay becalmed far out in the sea. The white sails fell motionless by the masts, and the sailors were whistling anxiously for a breeze. The captain gazed at the clouds with a wistful eye: "It will be a long while yet," muttered he, "before I see my dear wife, and kiss my little Polly and Bobby again."

"Oh dear, this state of things won't do," said the Wind; "they *must* get home soon; their stores are getting low, and their water is nearly out!" So he blew and blew a good steady breeze, and the white sails rounded out, while on went the gallant vessel like a steed obeying the rein, until the whitening waves flew on each side of her sharp bows. The sailors bustled about quite cheerily, and the captain walked up and down the deck, smiling to himself, and humming a cheerful sort of song that his little ones chaunted at home in their cosy house:—

"Blow, Wind, blow, and go ship, go,
In safety over the sea,
That Father may soon come home again,
Back to his babes and me!"

And the wind blew with such a will that the white cliffs and low green shores of his island home were soon to be seen; and the stately vessel glided safely and speedily into her harbour at last. Then did not the captain's wife cling round him, as if she never meant to let him go again? And the little children pulled his coat and shrieked with very joy that he was come home.

Then off went the wind once more; and he peeped into a school-room where some children were learning their lessons. By the open window stood Tom with an untouched sum on his slate, and he was looking as black as thunder. "If you don't do your lessons as a good boy should," whispered the wind, "I won't blow your kite one inch above the ground, nor sail your vessel in the pond either." Tom pouted and shrugged his shoulders. But the wind blew softly and steadily right in his face all the while: first tickling his nose, then peeping into his eyes, smoothing his cheeks, and then kissing his mouth, till at length and at last it blew away all Tom's ill tempers, so that he burst out laughing, and, taking up his slate, set to work with a hearty good-will until he had finished and proved his sum right.

"That was a good piece of work done," said the Wind, drawing a long breath after it; "and now the tide is rolling up, and the Rain will be coming in to compare notes: so I must be off to tell him all I have done!"

BIRDS.

SWALLOWS, Swallows, where have
you been?
Come hither and tell to me,
What are the wonders that you
have seen
In lands far over the sea.
Have you seen the graceful palm-trees grow
In the isles of the distant main,—
And the gorgeous flowers of the tropics bloom,
Ere you homeward turned again?"
But the swallows were building so busily,
They could not stop to gossip with me.

"Howlet, Howlet, night's coming on,
Tarry a moment with me,
And tell if your nest's in the tower of the
church,
Or built in a nice hollow tree.

Do you haunt at night the moss-thatched barn,
  A-hunting for sparrows and mice,
Well-fed on wheat, to your young they 'll prove
  A tempting morsel and nice!"
But the owl he blinked solemn and wise as he
    flew,
And all that he said was, "Tu whit, tu whoo!"

"Kingfisher, Kingfisher, golden and green,
  You sit on the bank of the stream;
Have you seen the old water-rat peep abroad,
  Or the silvery minnows gleam?
The dragon-fly poise on her slender wing,
  Like a fairy sprite at play:—
Of the living things in this limpid brook,
  Have you nothing at all to say?"
But the kingfisher flew, with a dart and a gleam,
  On a tiny fish in the rapid stream!

"Skylark, Skylark, soaring so high
  In the cloudless summer air,
What did you see in the deep blue sky,
  That looks so calm and so fair?

Were the stars asleep and folded up
In the fleecy cloudlet's breast,
While the pale moon watched above them all,
Like a mother o'er a nest?"
But the skylark was soaring up so high,
I lost her voice in the distant sky.

"Sea-gull, Sea-gull, sailing along,
From the shore of the sounding sea,
Will you fold for a moment your strong broad wing,
And bring some tidings to me?
Your music is ever the hollow roar,
Of the waves as they rise and fall,
And the ceaseless change of the ocean's face,
You have known and watched it all."
But the sea-gull paused not to answer me,
As he sailed away to his home by the sea.

"Birdies, Birdies, I'll ask no more,
For none of you answer me;
Go home to your roost in the rocky crag,
Or your nest in tower or tree;

For the fowler 's abroad and looking for prey,
 I hear the sound of his gun ;
He 'll never pause to hear what you say,
 So be off with you, every one.
He 'll ask no questions of where you have been,
Nor care a jot for the sights you have seen !

SHOWING HOW MINCE-PIES WERE INTRODUCED INTO CORNERWISE.

IN a very out-of-the-way country, in a remote part of the world, stood the quaint little town of Cornerwise. It had been noted, from very early time, for the remarkable wisdom of its inhabitants; and by its habitually rare contact with neighbouring cities, preserved, till a later period, its original sagacity. No dangerous innovations ever found their way into Cornerwise, for, with a noble simplicity, its citizens ate, drank, slept, and dressed, as their forefathers had done for generations before them. One or two daring spirits, more adventurous than the rest, had risked a little foreign travel, by visiting some of the neighbouring towns; but their conduct was unanimously looked upon with silent disapproval, and the innovations they sought to recommend, clamorously disallowed. For instance, when Master Peer, the barber, paid his celebrated visit to his seventieth cousin ten times removed, who resided in the adjacent town of Advanceall, he actually had the audacity to come home brimful of a new project for lighting his native city; and even went the length of proposing it in full town council, before the mayor and aldermen! But they magnanimously and calmly overlooked the matter; telling him, with great forbearance, that Cornerwise had always been illuminated by small oil lamps suspended across the streets; and that they, being in their sober senses, would sanction no such dangerous innovations as inflammable vapours, which must be injurious to public health, and, moreover, sounded so improbable as to savour of magic. Wherefore they advised Master Peer, as an orderly citizen, to retire to his own home, and go through a course of sedative medicine; and they, being kindly disposed, would consign the matter to oblivion. Whereon Master Peer did go home, and either from suppressed rage or the native physic, became ill, and on his recovery found his rival had obtained all his business, and succeeded him in the care of the pigtails of the whole corporation. Then poor Master Peer pined away, and becoming an object of scorn to the town boys, who called after him, "There's the man who wanted to set the air on fire!" retired utterly to private life—that is, his bed—being a notable warning to all the wild spirits of Cornerwise.

Then there was the unfortunate Martha Trippitt, who happening, in a somewhat extended walk beyond the city walls, to fall in with a damsel of the town of Smartingale, was desperately infected with the love of imitation. So she ran home again and secretly stole one of the hoops off her mother's flour-tub, to put in her petticoat, that her dress might be as like a balloon as could be. But the virtuous indignation of all the little boys in Cornerwise was aroused, and they hooted and called after her so, that she did not dare set her foot out of doors. Then she fell into a hopeless state of melancholy and died, leaving orders with her disconsolate relatives, that she should be buried in her hoop.

And after these two serious warnings, the people of Cornerwise, with their magistrates at their head, were more opposed than ever to improvement. At this time it was, that, to the great edification of the citizens, the motto was re-cut deeper and larger over the Town-hall—"Stand still." Moreover, an edict was passed in full town council, setting forth that the town of Cornerwise disowned all amendments and improvements; and that those malicious and evil-disposed persons who sought to introduce such changes, would be from henceforth liable to the severest penalties of the law.

Now, in one of the obscure back-lanes of Cornerwise lived an old widow,—a solitary woman, for her kinsfolk were dead, and she had no known relatives in the town. Of a large family of children, there only remained one representative, in the person of her grandson, Jack. He was a fine, stout, curly-pated urchin, who was at once the delight and the torment of his poor old grandmother. He was very good at his lessons, and loved her dearly; but he was so mischievous and full of tricks, that she had no peace of mind when he was out of her sight. He was the chief of all the unruly spirits in Cornerwise, the ringleader of every prank, and the plotter of all kinds of ingenious mischief. He it was who drove a long nail through the hands of the clock at the Town-hall, and painted on it in large red letters the town motto—"Stand still." It was also shrewdly suspected, that he was the cause of Cornerwise being barricaded in its own citadel, by the stuffing-up of the key-holes of the city gates with clay, and the inscription of the same startling motto on the inside. He crowned his offences by enlisting the services of his ragamuffin crew, and by their aid, tied every weathercock fast north and south, and stopped all the clocks in the town, so that the mayor was obliged to despatch a messenger ten miles off to the next village, to ask which way the wind blew!

After this last performance, Jack was obliged to remain quiet for a while, for, although it could not be exactly traced home to him, the authorities were pretty well aware who the chief culprit really was; so that had not Jack's band of conspirators included the boys of the corporation, and even the eldest son of the mayor himself, his stay in Cornerwise would have been somewhat brief. Besides, with all his sins, he was a tender-hearted fellow, and he did not like to see his grandmother sit crying, and vowing he would break her heart if he went on with his naughty tricks any more.

So he went up to bed with his supper, a dry crust of bread, in a rather more sober humour than usual. He slept in a little garret, with a window overlooking the town-wall, so that he could see the road and fields beyond. While he was munching his hard morsel, and musing over his misdeeds, he chanced to look down into the road that wound below, when he became aware of a man who was sitting on the mile-stone with a large box beside him. Then the man began to sing in a loud voice, and his ditty ran thus :—

"Apples and currants, sugar and spice,
Brandy and lemon, candied-peel nice.
All these good things go to make mince-pies!"

"Mince-pies!" thought Jack, "what are they, I wonder? Can they be like those great gooseberry-pies Granny makes?"

Jack was not a boy to miss knowledge for want of asking, so he called to the man, and asked what he meant by his song, and what mince-pies were made of.

"Why, don't I tell you?" replied the man very briskly; "Can't you hear :—

'Apples and currants, sugar and spice,
Brandy and lemon, candied-peel nice.'

That's what we make mince-pies of. But do you mean to say you never tasted them?"

"No," said Jack, "I have lived all my life in

Cornerwise, but I never heard of mince-pies before!"

"Poor fellow," answered the pieman, "no wonder you are so ignorant if you have lived here all your days. But as you seem a lively sort of young boy, if you will let down a string I will send you up a bit to taste."

Jack, highly delighted, thanked the man very gratefully, and routing out a long piece of string from among his hoards of such-like treasures, he weighted it with an old broken top, and let it down carefully out of the window.

Now the man stood close by the edge of the road, just under the window, and when he took the lid off his green box, a delicious odour mounted up in the air and made Jack's mouth water. It was not exactly like a smell of flowers, or fruits, or spices, or pastry, but such a mingled combination of all four, that it seemed a waft of the air of Fairyland to Jack, who, like all boys of his age, had a keen relish for tarts and pies; a liking much enhanced by the rarity with which they fell to his share. When the pieman had carefully fixed the pie on the string, Jack eagerly, but tenderly, drew it up, watching and guarding it most heedfully against any rough angle or corner of the wall. Up, up, up, brick after brick,—past cranny and crevice,—up, up, till it reached the window safe at last, and lay on the sill in all its glory, before Jack's admiring eyes. Round as a daisy, brown as a bee, wrinkled and puckered all over in the most tempting dimples, and varnished till it was as shiny as the petal of a buttercup! Jack gazed at it in such an ecstasy of admiration that he almost forgot it was meant to be eaten. He lifted the lid and peeped in! oh what a conglomeration of richness and daintiness was there! plump currants, luscious sweets, long transparent slices of golden peel, lumps of apple! Jack's heart was in his mouth, and the pie too, before he even remembered to thank the pieman.

"Sugar and spice!" murmured Jack, "and all that's nice!" as he waxed even poetical under the influence of the delicious morsel, "apples and currants, oh!—Brandy and lemon, ah!—

THE PIEMAN AND JACK OF CORNERWISE.

Page 90.

Mince pies!—Why I should think the fairies lived on them!"

"How do you like mince pies?" asked the pieman, who was tired of waiting so long.

"I never tasted anything so good before in my life!" cried Jack enthusiastically, "what a man you must be to make them! Oh dear me, there goes the last bit. You have not any more, have you?"

"Not to-day," answered the man; "but I will bring you one every evening about this time, only you must promise not to tell any one, as it might get me into a scrape with the good people of Cornerwise!"

Of course Jack promised eagerly, and the pieman, shouldering his box, from which, while he lifted the corner of the lid, a last exquisite whiff curled up in the evening air, and ascended to Jack's nose, he took his departure. Jack's eyes followed him as he strode away towards the dim blue hills, his lengthening shadow falling far behind him, till he was lost in the distance. You may be sure the boy's visions that night were of beneficent piemen and ambrosial pies. He dreamed that he was transported to a delighful country, where the mince pies grew on the bushes, and called after him—

> "Apples and currants, sugar and spice,
> Brandy and lemon, candied-peel nice,
> Come and eat us,—mince-pies—mince-pies!"

Next morning he overslept himself, and was so late that his poor old grandmother hobbled up stairs to wake him, and shook him in a great fright.

"Yes, Granny, sugar and spice! coming directly; brandy—and shoes—where are my mince pies—I mean my clothes?"

"Bless the boy! what's he talking about?" said Granny, "pies, child, we haven't had any pies for many a day!"

Jack dressed himself and had his breakfast, but the mince-pies still ran in his head and intruded in his conversation. He made all sorts of mistakes in his confusion; for he remembered the pieman's warning, and tried to check himself, which only made matters worse.

He went out into the market-place, hoping to divert his mind; but there he met the Mayor, who being in an unusually amiable mood, meant to be very graciously forgiving to Jack, by asking him what o'clock it was.

"Apples and currants, sugar and spice!" answered Jack, readily. The Mayor, who thought he meant to be saucy, angrily reproved him, and moreover boxed his ears till they tingled again. Then Madam March dropped her gold-headed cane and called Jack to pick it up for her.

"To be sure," said Jack. "Brandy and lemon, sugar and spice!"

"You audacious boy," screamed the old lady, vindictively, "I'll get his Worship to set you in the stocks, for mocking your betters!"

Endless were the scrapes Jack got into, and numerous the cuffs he received: for what with his constantly recurring thoughts of the mince-pies, and his anxiety not to betray himself, he did not escape as he usually did from the consequences of his misdeeds. The evening came, the pieman and the pie! and again did Jack revel in the delicious dainty, this time, however, reserving a share for a favourite comrade. It cost him no small self-denial to refrain from eating it; and if his eyes could have devoured it, I am afraid his friend would have had a small share. However, Jack magnanimously abstained, and the cherished dainty was bestowed on the boy, with a strict injunction to secresy. When two become joint possessors of a secret, it is pretty sure to ooze out somewhere; and the absence of mind of both Jack and his friend, and their several rambling and incoherent allusions to

"Apples and currants, sugar and spice,
Brandy and lemon, candied-peel nice,"

spread far and wide among the juvenile population of Cornerwise. The Mayor's son, among others, was taken into the secret, and obtained a surreptitious taste of the pies.

Now whether there was, as the Cornerwise matrons afterwards averred, some evil-designed magical agent in this mysterious compound, there is at this present time no means of discovering. Certain it is, however, that all who tasted of the coveted dainty, became imbued with a frantic longing for more; and the pieman, finding his admirers increase to such a large body, informed them that he could no longer supply them gratuitously, but that he should be happy to furnish any amount of supply for a moderate price, if they could procure him a suitable shop for selling them. Then did the hearts of the bold youth of Cornerwise, inflamed by the pies, burn within them, and they determined on a bold stroke for the mastery.

Accordingly, on the following day, when the town council were in full sitting, the sons and heirs of the worshipful corporation and burghers assembled at the widow's house, and forming in martial order they marched to the town-hall in a large procession, with Jack at their head, bearing a huge banner, inscribed with the word "Forward," and followed by the pieman in full dress, white apron and cook's cap, bearing the insignia of his order, the paste-board and rolling-pin. Then followed the youthful representatives of every house in Cornerwise, carrying mince-pies, out of which they took a huge bite at stated signals. The whole band shouted in chorus the mystical words, that had puzzled everybody so long:—

> "Apples and currants, sugar and spice,
> Brandy and lemon, candied-peel nice,
> We will, WE SHALL, WE MUST have mince pies!"

When they reached the town-hall, a large deputation, headed by the principal agitators, waited on the astonished magistrates, and demanded the repeal of the obnoxious old statute, as well as a new enactment regulating the sale of mince pies in Cornerwise. The Mayor was inclined to take the matter with a high hand, and consign the heads of the mob to durance vile, but on the hint of such an intention, such a clamour arose, and such shouts of "Reform," "Progress," "Free Trade," and other democratic cries were heard, that the Corporation prevailed on him to give the juvenile malcontents a calmer hearing. Rumour, who has always the last word to say about anybody, affirms that the outcry drew out the matrons of the town, and that they, naturally anxious for the welfare of their young hopefuls, took such a decided part in the municipal counsels, that a compromise was finally agreed to. The said Rumour, who is not "painted all over tongues" for nothing, also hinted that the Mayoress, perhaps incited thereto by a sly morsel of the felonious dainty, secretly administered by her son, took the Mayor aside for a very private conference, and by some especially strong and striking arguments, won him over to her view of the state of the case.

So the matter ended, by its being enacted in solemn council, then and there assembled, that the compound, entitled mince-pies, should be from that time forward a lawful and staple commodity in Cornerwise, being, however, strictly, for reasons prudential, confined to the high festival of Christmas, and all the days thereunto appertaining. And a licence was given to the pieman aforesaid, to establish a place of abode in the town for the manufacture and sale of the article, the chief magistrates of the town having always a prior selection from his wares.

Then there arose great rejoicing in the ancient borough of Cornerwise, and, after the custom of consistent magistrates, the Mayor and Corporation lunched so very amply on the novel viands that they were obliged to retire into seclusion for a few days to recover.

Years passed over the little town, and Jack became a thriving and prosperous man; for the grateful pieman, owing his establishment in Cornerwise to him, had given him a partnership in his business. In time he rose to high offices in his native town, finally becoming Mayor of Cornerwise. In grateful appreciation of the many benefits he had conferred on the town, his fellow-citizens placed a statue of him in the market-place, attired in his civic robes, and with a mince-pie in his hand. Underneath, this quaint legend may still be deciphered by those who are fortunate enough to go to Cornerwise,—

"Lyttel Jacke Horner sate inne ye Corner,
Eating a Christe-Masse Pye,
Hee putte inne hys Thumbe,
And pulled oute a Plumbe,
And cryed 'What a goode Ladde am I!'"

After this famous occurrence, however, Cornerwise became a different place. Sometimes when something or other makes a little hole in a hedge, other things pass through, and the hole widens into a breach. And so it was with our Cornerwise: one cherished abuse after another became swept away in the great stream of time; so that it is now so practical and commonplace a little town, that you would not know it if you found yourself in it.

THE SORROWS OF SPINNIKIN.

MY dear," said the old Spider to her youngest child, "you will never get on in the world if you don't take more pains."

"Oh never mind me, mamma," remarked the hopeful Spiderling; "I daresay I shall get on somehow; and, at any rate, I don't mean to trouble my head about it yet. I don't care!"

"You don't know the end 'Don't Care' came to, I daresay," replied her mother; "do you know he was hanged?"

"Well, that is what happens to me every day of my life," remarked the Spider pertly, "when you cut off my thread, down I must come head-foremost; and it is lucky my brains are easily reversible!"

The old Spider shrugged up her shoulders in

despair and went off to her net, while the thoughtless "Spinnikin" sat comfortably down in a corner to discuss the cold remains of a bee.

"Oh Spinnikin, Spinnikin!" cried her mother, from the top bud of a high hollyhock, "you don't call this neat work, do you? Every bit of it will have to be picked out again. Why, here is not a straight line in it; and your rounds are more like squares!"

"Never mind," said Spinnikin, "I am not fond of net-making. I like to enjoy myself, and I shall do it until I am obliged to get settled in life. I like scrambling up and down the stalks, and swinging from the top of the branches; and then there's always plenty of cold fly in the larder!"

"And, pray, who provides it?" inquired the old Spider severely. "When I was your age I was forced to make my own nets, and the experience of many a hungry day taught me to make them well, too! But what is to become of you when I am gone I can't think."

"Never mind now," answered Spinnikin, "I

don't care. Come and taste some of the bee, I can tell you it's uncommonly tender and sweet!"

And then when Spinnikin had finished her lunch, she went to the end of the hollyhock bough, and let herself down by the help of a thread; and her friend, the Breeze, came up to play with her, and he swung her till she was so tired she could hardly climb up again.

"You won't have quite so much time for such frolics one of these days!" remarked a a spiteful Cockchafer, who sat grinning at her from a sunflower growing near.

"I don't care" sang Spinnikin, "I'm very fond of play, and I'll have it while I can get it; and as for the rest, let the future take care of itself. There is always plenty of food in the larder for me!"

"I daresay you are happy enough now," said the Cockchafer, "because it is May, and the sun shines, and the flowers are all open. But winter is coming; oh yes! winter is coming, and the cold weather and the rain. What will you do then?"

"What I do now," answered Spinnikin tartly, for she did not relish his rude observations. "Curl myself under a leaf to be sure!"

"Ah, ha! but there will be no leaves for you then," laughed he, "nothing but bare branches, ha, ha! Miss Spinnikin!"

Spinnikin was very angry and rather uncomfortable; but as she did not know how to answer him, she turned her back on him and went away.

Alas for Spinnikin! her happiest days seemed to be over, and her ill fortune to commence from that date. First of all, her indulgent mother met her death in a terribly violent and sudden manner, for she was chumped up by a voracious donkey, with the green plant she had made her home, and consequently the larder was full no longer. Spinnikin who never took pains with anything, constructed her nets in such a "gobblestitch" manner, that everything was *not* "fish" that came into them. Big Bluebottles buzzed over them and under them, and little flies crept through them; but neither stopped on the way to form food for poor Spinnikin. So she earned a somewhat precarious living by chance, and was often reduced to very stale legs and wings, that in her former prosperous days she had left in a despised corner of the tattered old web. Sometimes her relatives would, from motives of charity, bestow a stray gnat or a skinny harvest-man upon her; but they accompanied their lean presents with such unpleasant remarks, that poor Spinnikin would almost as soon have gone hungry.

And now the chilly Autumn days came on, and the gnats and bees were very few and far between; and, as the Cockchafer had foretold, the cold biting winds robbed her green bower of the sheltering leaves, so that when showers of rain or hail-storms came on, poor Spinnikin was sadly put to it to find a shelter.

At last one day when she had been hunting about in vain for a stray morsel, a bright thought entered her little head; for necessity frequently sharpens people's wits and brings out their dormant qualities. She had often climbed up to the very top of the hollyhock (now shorn of all its handsome red flowers), and she had peeped from thence into the open window belonging to a house that stood hard by.

"What should hinder me from making it my winter residence?" said Spinnikin. "Such a charming home as it must be, air and water-tight, and warm besides. No sooner said than done. She climbed to the top of her friendly hollyhock, and taking advantage of a useful puff of wind, she landed safely on the sill of the window, and entered upon a new course of life as a house spider.

But poor Spinnikin found that mere outside show is not always to be trusted, and she discovered that living inside a house with all its advantages, had also its drawbacks. She missed the pretty green that used to shelter her, and the nice bud branches on which she made her nets. Her mother's lessons came sadly back to her recollection, as she tried in her bungling manner to fix her foundation threads on slippery painted edges and smooth glass.

Then there were perils and dangers to look for; every day the maid came in with an awful long broom, with which she swept wall and window for stray cobwebs. Many of poor Spinnikin's "gobblestitch" webs were carried away in this manner, before she had even had a chance of entrapping the few sleepy flies that buzzed about the window frames. Indeed, she found it necessary to be remarkably active to escape being swept away herself, and she was obliged to rush up her ladders and hide trembling in a secret corner, till the formidable broom had passed by. Many a hair-breadth escape had she; but from continual use she became almost accustomed to her danger.

One day she had been incessantly persecuted, by the housemaid and the broom, who both seemed possessed of a particular fit of cleanliness that day, and mutually poked out every hole and corner three times over. However, Spinnikin passed safely through this ordeal; and, having watched them safely out of the room, she set to work again, and hastily spun her web as usual; but whether it was because she was nervous and unsteady from the perils she had passed, or whether she set to work, as her old mother used to tell her, without taking pains, it is impossible to say. Certain it is, however, that her web was by no means secure, and it was not materially benefited by the fat paws of a troublesome kitten, who came to the window to try and catch flies.

Spinnikin was sitting in her corner watching her nets as usual, when she saw a remarkably fine Blue Bottle fly caught by one wing in her toils. Eager and excited by the sight, Spinnikin made a dart and sprung to pounce on her prey, but her frail footing gave way, and down she went into a deep basin of water that stood underneath, and from which her thread could not help her to escape. "Oh! had I only mended that rent in my Cobweb," groaned Spinnikin, "I should not have come here!"

But it was useless to regret this now,—she had disregarded her mother's advice, till her careless habits had so grown upon her, they had become second nature. Poor Spinnikin had never taken pains with anything she had done, she had always trusted to get out of the scrape somehow. And thus she met her fate in a watery grave; and "Don't Care" for once, in lieu of coming to be hanged, was drowned instead. And heedless Spinnikin and her sorrows came to an end together.

MORAL.

Little folks, mind what your mothers say to you, and don't make "Gobblestitches!"

THE BALLAD

OF

PATTY PERIWINKLE.

I'D like to be a Dahlia!"
Said Patty Periwinkle,
"To have a grand red velvet gown,
"With many a fold and wrinkle.

"I'd like to be a Dahlia!
"So tall and lofty growing,
"And with my large green spreading leaves,
"About me full and flowing!

"I'd like to be a Dahlia!
"My lofty blossom raising,
"With such a grand majestic air,
"To woo the sunbeam's praising.

"The trees should bend above me,
"The blossoms bow before me,
"The bee respect my golden heart,
"The butterfly adore me:

"The speckled thrush at evening
"With songs of love address me,
"The gentle airs, in dallyings soft,
"Should welcome and caress me.

"The brook should chaunt my praises,
"In many a merry tinkle,
"I wish I was a Dahlia!"
Sighed Patty Periwinkle.

She grew quite discontented,
With all who came unto her,—
She snubbed the snail, she flapped the fly,
Because they dared to woo her.

She would not kiss the cricket,
Or gossip with the daisy,—
These little people stared at her,
And fancied she was crazy.

And while her airs and graces
  Her neighbours all were flouting,
A saucy sun-ray glinted down,
  To show how she was pouting.

The green leaves and the grasses tall,
  Shook with ringing laughter
Of all who heard her discontent—
  And saw what followed after!

Then said an old Blue-Bottle—
  "You're neither wise nor witty,
"To tire of your blue petticoat,
  "So delicately pretty!

"The Dahlia sports a crimson robe,
  "Her rank is far above you:
"Why covet you her rich attire,
  "When you've such hosts to love you?"

"I daresay all you tell is true!"
  Sighed Patty Periwinkle,
"But oh! that crimson robe 's so rich
  "With many a fold and wrinkle!"

"Ha! ha!" laughed out the Earwig,
(To speak he scarce was able,)
"The Dahlia grand you knew last year,
"Is but a stick and label!

"Her root 's so large and juicy,
"(Both rain and sun did pet her,)
"That I, and all my hungry tribe
"So loved her,—that we ate her!"

Then through the grass and leaves again
There rang a merry titter,
Poor Patty Periwinkle felt
In a most awful twitter!

But all the sense, that in her heart
Lay folded up and hidden,
At reason's voice, so clear and strong,
Came boldly forth unbidden.

"I'd rather have my pale blue gown,
"Without a fold or wrinkle!
"Than merely make an earwig's meal!"
Quoth Patty Periwinkle.

FRITZ AND HIS FRIENDS.

ONCE upon a time, there was a poor old woman who lived in a little hut, close to the edge of a vast forest, that stretched away many miles and ended no one knew where. She lived in great poverty, so great indeed, that it was all she could do to find just bread enough to live upon for herself and her son, a fine, tall lad. He did what he could to support his mother; but still it could not be very much, for there was no town near, where he could obtain work. So all that he could do, was to labour hard at their little garden, which by severe toil he had succeeded in clearing and reclaiming from the forest. Here grew a few beans and lentils, some common pot-herbs and simples; and there was a tiny patch of barley, which found them in bread.

This year, however, great misfortunes befel them; the winter had been terribly severe, and the living creatures in the forest had been almost starved. One day, when he came to look at the barley he had just sown, he found the ground all marked with the print of little feet, and the seed evidently picked out. He was much vexed at this, and determined to set a trap to catch the thief. This he accordingly did, and then went home to his mother to tell her the misfortune that had happened to him, which was all the worse that he had no more seed barley to sow.

Next morning he went eagerly to examine his trap, and on looking in, perceived that he had been successful; there was a pretty wood-pigeon, with its feathers all ruffled and puffed up, sitting in one corner. "Ah ha! little thief!" said Fritz, "so I have caught you! Now I will make you pay for eating my barley!" The poor thing looked at him piteously with its soft dark eyes, as if pleading to him to spare its life. Fritz felt his heart relent as he looked at it.

"I have a great mind to let you go now," said he; "I should think the fright was almost punishment enough!" The pigeon seemed to understand him, for it smoothed down its feathers and crept towards him, gazing gently in his face. "Here goes then," said Fritz, opening the door of the trap; "be off with you; only mind you don't come stealing my barley any more, or I won't promise not to make a pie of you next time!" The pigeon flew on his shoulder and kissed him very softly with her bill, as if to thank him for her liberty; and then spreading her wings, off she flew to the forest.

"It was no good to take the poor creature's life," said Fritz. "I suppose her hunger drove her to it, and I know what that is myself; but," he added ruefully, "that won't put back my barley though. But I suppose I must take double care of the beans and lentils."

So saying, he walked off to the little garden plot, where they were planted. They were coming up nicely, and just showing their green tops above the ground when he visited them last, so he hoped to see them quite flourishing. To his horror he found them all eaten off close to the earth, and his crop totally destroyed. So down he put the trap he had brought from the barley-field, hoping to catch this thief also. Next morning he returned, and peeping into it, he saw soft white fur, and long ears, but the bright eyes were hidden in great terror.

"Oh ho," said Fritz, "it's you, Bunny, is it! And a very pretty creature you are, with all your wicked doings!"

And so she was, for she was snow-white, without blemish or spot, with large long ears, and lovely bright eyes.

"Well," said Fritz, "Your know your fate, Bunny; the best thing I can do with you is to roast you and eat you, to make up for the mischief you have done!"

The poor little rabbit sat up and held out its

fore-paws, as if begging for mercy. Fritz's heart was somewhat easily touched, so he let the pretty rabbit go; consoling himself with the idea, that after all it was only fair, as he had forgiven the wood-pigeon before. Away skipped the rabbit into the wood, giving a merry whisk with her short tail, by way of a farewell.

Then Fritz went back to his poor cottage, and his mother asked him what news he had of the crops. The old woman was terribly vexed when she heard the real truth.

"Oh Fritz, my child," said she, "what shall we do for bread?"

"Well, mother," said Fritz, "If I had brought you home both the pigeon and the rabbit, they would but have served two meals, and that would not have bettered us much."

The next day, as Fritz was wandering dolefully in the forest, and pondering in his mind how to make both ends meet, he heard a great sound of tramping feet, and on looking carefully about, he saw in the distance shining arms and waving plumes glimmering among the trees. When he came near to them, he found they were a regiment of soldiers who were going to encamp in the forest, and who were seeking a suitable camp. Fritz told the commanding officer that he could guide them to a very nice place, where they would find plenty of wood and water. The officer was delighted to find a guide in so remote a spot; and as his men were utterly wearied with their long day's travel, he promised Fritz a substantial reward. Then Fritz took them to a safe and sequestered spot, where a good high wall of rock rose behind them, and formed a safe shelter from the wind and their enemies; and a nice clear stream flowed in front, supplying their wants, and offering another point of safety.

"And now," said the officer, "there is one more want you can perhaps supply. We are in great need of a safe and skilful messenger, who will carry a note to our allies. But the distance to be travelled is very long, and the road lies through a country swarming with adverse people. Still, the necessity for communication with our main army is so pressing, that I shall be empowered to offer vast advantages and rewards to whoever undertakes the task. The risk, I do not conceal from you, is very great, for if the messenger be taken he is sure to be shot."

Fritz was rather disheartened by this account of the difficulties and dangers he was to encounter; but the promised reward would keep his mother in comfort for the rest of her days. So he promised to think over the matter, and bring an answer in an hour's time. As he was sauntering sorrowfully in the forest, turning the affair over in his mind, something touched his foot. When he looked down he saw the soft white fur, and large ears of the pretty thief who had eaten his peas.

"What is the matter with you, my friend?" asked Bunny, in the most consequential way in the world.

"You can't help me, Bunny," laughed Fritz. "I dare say you can manage to eat other people's beans and peas quickly enough, but this is beyond your power!"

"How do you know," said Bunny, "till I tell you whether I can help you or not? At least, you might answer a civil question, and relate what ails you."

Then Fritz sat down among the fern, and told the rabbit all the story; and Bunny sat up and stroked her right ear with the most sagacious air in the world, and listened to his troubles.

"I'll be your messenger," said she, when Fritz had finished; "I can creep through holes, and scramble through hedges far easier than you can, and be less likely to be seen, too. So fetch me the note, and I'll tuck it into my left ear, and be off on my travels. I owe you a good turn for having eaten up all your beans and peas; and you gave me my life when it was in your power; if they shoot me, it will be but one poor Bunny less in the world, and some one will sup off rabbit, that's all!"

So the note was fetched; and the rabbit

FRITZ AND THE RABBIT.

Page 120.

stuck it very safely into her long left ear, where it was quite hid among her soft fur, and giving Fritz a merry parting nod, started off on her journey.

Three long days passed slowly by, every hour counted by Fritz with the greatest impatience. But, on the third evening, just as it was getting dusk, up limped poor Bunny with the answer.

"I should have been here before," said she, "but I had the misfortune to fall into a trap on my road, from which I only escaped with the loss of a good deal of fur, and at the expense of a lame leg."

And indeed the poor thing's leg was terribly bruised and mangled. Fritz took the note to the officer, received the proffered reward, and then carried his faithful little messenger home to his own cottage, where his mother bathed and bandaged the hurt poor Bunny had received in their service, and nursed her till she was quite cured.

One day, as Fritz was sitting by the door, playing with the little rabbit, his friend the officer came in, and after they had bidden each other good day, he proceeded to tell Fritz that he needed a faithful messenger once more, to warn the general of some secret intelligence he had gained, by which their enemies might fall into his hands.

"Alas!" replied Fritz, "I fear I am helpless to do anything for you now, as you see my poor faithful little carrier is disabled, but I will see what can be done before eventide."

Then the officer departed, after telling him that the message was so important, the bearer might claim any reward he chose.

"Let me try and take the letter," said Bunny, hopping up from her basket, "I dare say I can manage to scramble on that distance."

"No, no, my poor little faithful darling," said Fritz, "you have met with troubles enough already in my service; besides time is a matter of such importance, now."

At this moment Fritz heard a little tap, tap, at the window; and, on opening it, saw the pretty pigeon he had released from his trap.

"Good day, Fritz," cooed the pretty creature, caressing him with her soft bill, "but what is the matter, my friend, you seem in trouble?"

Fritz told her how he had sent the rabbit with the message, and the misfortune he had met with, so that he was now at a loss what to do.

"Is that all," said the Pigeon, "give the note to me, or rather tie it under my wing: and I will fly there and back in two or three hours, and escape all the dangers by the way."

Then Fritz, in great delight, ran off to his friend the officer, and having obtained from him the important letter, he carefully tied it under the pigeon's wing. She spread her glossy wings, and with a parting nod to Fritz, away she soared into the blue air, lessening every moment, until she became a mere speck, and was then lost to sight altogether.

Fritz, and the officer too, watched most anxiously for her return, but hour after hour passed by and still no pigeon. Night came, dark and tempestuous, and the captain returned to his camp, giving up the messenger for lost. By and by, Fritz heard a faint tap at the window, and, rushing to open it, he drew in the poor little pigeon, ruffled and wet, and so weary she could not speak. When he drew her to the light, he found she was covered with blood. The note that was tied under her wing was sprinkled with the life-stream that was flowing from her soft wounded bosom.

"My pretty creature," said Fritz, "I had far rather have lost the reward than have gained it at the expense of your life."

The poor little thing fluttered her feathers feebly, tried to touch his hand with her beak, but the bright eyes closed, and she expired. Very sore was Fritz's heart for the loss of his faithful messenger—the pretty creature who had laid down her life in his service.

The intelligence, however, she had so faithfully gained was of the utmost service to the army, and the grateful captain lost no time in placing the claims of Fritz before the King, who appointed him an officer in his army; but though he rose in time to great honour and riches, Fritz never lost his old kindness and humanity; and to him many a poor criminal owed his reprieve. His old mother lived all the rest of her life in the utmost luxury, tenderly cared-for by her affectionate son. And Fritz grew in course of time to be a general and a great man; he had large estates and gave grand entertainments. He took for his crest a carrier pigeon; and when he was asked the reason why, he used to tell the story of the gratitude of the rabbit and the pigeon.

"No friends are too small to be of good service!" said Fritz. "Never despise love or friendship, in however small or mean disguise it may come, or perhaps you may send away angels, unawares!"

TIDINGS OF SPRING.

ART thou peeping from the snow,
Little bud of the flower?
From thy rest so long and deep,
Art thou roused up every hour,
By the warmth that seems to shoot
From the sun down to the root?
Little bud! little bud! it is time thou wert awake.

"I am coming to the light;
Every leaflet creeping up,
Little child, was folded tight
In the sheath of my green cup,
And the dew, the sun, the air,
In my veins thrill everywhere.
Little child! little child! I am waking up at last!"

Art thou stirring in the hive,
  Bonny bee, busy bee?
It is time thou wert alive;
  For the flowers are blooming free,—
And the lovely Spring is coming
With her honey; art thou humming?
Busy bee, busy bee? it is time thou wert
    abroad.

"I am ready for my toil!
  In the Spring-tide's early dawn,
Shall I seek my fragrant spoil
  In the dewy air of morn;
Never idle, never dreary,
Sunny morn, or evening, weary.
Little child! little child! I am labouring for
    thee!"

Art thou building up thy nest,
  Little bird? Hast thou come
To spread thy loving breast
  O'er the speckled eggs at home?

Art thou seeking twigs and hair,
Moss and wool round everywhere?
Little bird! little bird! it is time thou wert at work.

"We are building on the bough,
Little child, we come to thee;
Weary wanderers are we now,
From the lands beyond the sea;
And we search about for food
To supply the infant brood,
Who in June, very soon, will be chirping in the nest!"

Art thou coming with the Spring,
Little lamb to the lea?
Where the daisies in a ring
Gather round to welcome thee,
See the tender grasses grow
All the fresher for the snow.
Green again, is the plain, and the leaf is on the tree.

"Skipping fleetly o'er the lea,
  Little maiden, here am I.
And I gambol fast and free,
  And close nestled-up I lie
By my soft and gentle mother,
For we, too, love one another.
Little maid, little maid! I love spring as much
    as thou!"

"I've been folded in the nest,
  Fed and sheltered tenderly
In my loving parent's breast,
  Bee and bird, as well as ye.
We are all young things together,
In the pleasant spring-time weather.
Playmates all, playmates all, and all little
    friends are we!"

MINA'S DREAM.

MINA had a holiday!

For a long while, she had been exceedingly good in learning her lessons: she had filled her copy-book with the neatest writing possible; she had learned a new French verb, and worked mamma a charming pair of slippers. So, at last, she had fairly earned her long-promised holiday; and cousin Carrie was coming to spend the day with her! In honour of the occasion, the doll's dinner and tea-service were to be used; and a bountiful provision of cake and fruit had been given her by her mamma. They were to play in the green shady bower, formed by the drooping branches of the weeping ash, where already the doll had been installed in her smart cradle of pink and white.

In short, Mina had made up her mind to enjoy her holiday to the very utmost. When she went to bed the night before, she could scarcely sleep for thinking of all the delightful things she meant to do on that happiest of days. But, alas! for all short-sighted plans—those of little people are as apt to miscarry as those of the great folks. When Mina opened her great blue eyes in the morning, instead of being greeted with a warm kiss from the bright sun, she only saw cold grey skies, and heard the drip, drip, dripping of the steady rain.

"Oh dear, dear!" said Mina dolefully, "how provoking of that horrid rain, to choose this day of all others—

'Rain, Rain, go to Spain,
Fair weather come again!'"

But Mina's charmed rhyme took no effect on the great black clouds overhead; and they steadily poured down a deluge. Patter, patter, went the rain-drops; trickle, trickle, came the little rills of water down the window-panes.

"Perhaps it will clear up before twelve o'clock!" said Mina hopefully.

So she dressed, and ate her breakfast with a fair share of resignation. But ten, eleven, twelve, were chimed in succession by the clock in the hall, and still no abatement of the steady rain. Mina had somewhat mournfully taken up her station at the window; and she watched the pools of water in the gravel-walk, as they rippled and dimpled beneath the fall of the rain-drops. Her mamma advised her to go into the hall and play battle-dore and shuttle-cock, or to practise her music-lesson: but Mina was by this time very much out of temper, and did not feel inclined to be either amiable or easily amused. She teased the cat, till pussy scratched her arm; and worried Shock, till he barked at her, and brought her brother out to see what was the reason of the unusual excitement of his dog.

When her early dinner was ready, and she was summoned to the school-room, she was very rude and pert to old Mary, the nurse, who had watched over her from her cradle; and was utterly disdainful of the cakes and fruit her mamma had provided for her dessert. So Mary looked at her through her spectacles, and said: "Miss Mina, you have put the wrong foot out of bed this morning, my dear; and all because it rains!"

Now Mina had been very cross, and, consequently, very miserable, all the whole morning; and so nurse's undeserved kind words, and her hand laid gently on the pettish little shoulder, so wilfully shrugged up, opened the flood-gates of her heart, and set her tears flowing as fast as the rain. She was ashamed to show it, however, and so off she flew to her favourite hiding-place. This was a large bay-window in the drawing-room, protected by wide sheltering curtains; and here she ensconced herself with a couple of cushions, and sat down to meditate over her unfortunate holiday. She cuddled her little fat arms up in her frock, and rolled herself up in the warm Siberian blanket from the sofa; and by the aid of these coverings and tuckings up, and after rocking backwards and forwards a little, her tears ceased, and her blue eyes quietly closed. She was asleep; and the nice good fairy, who weaves little children's dreams, must by chance have been passing that way, and sent one to Mina. And this was the substance of her dream.

She thought she was travelling through a pleasant lane, divided from broad corn-fields on either side by a low green hedge, rich with wild flowers. Presently, she came to a gate which led into the wheat-field, through which she passed. The golden corn stood up in tall spears on each side of her; while, like jewels in a rich setting, gleamed here and there among them, the scarlet poppy, the azure corn-flower, and the pale purple scabious. But the poppy looked faded and wrinkled, the corn-flower was closed, and screwed up, and the slender stalk of the scabious could not support its heavy head; while the golden ears of the ripe corn drooped and hung down wearily. The bright sun-rays seemed to scorch and burn them all, instead of smiling on them, and drawing them up to cheerful life.

"Poor things," said Mina, compassionately, "you all look very pining; what is the matter?"

"Oh," replied the Poppy, "can you give us a drop of water to drink? We are dying with thirst." "Our roots are dried up in the parched earth," sighed the Corn, wearily; "our strength is fast failing—we are perishing of drought."

"I cannot help you," replied Mina, "for there is no water near,—not even enough for a draught for the Poppy!"

Then the Corn nodded a faint adieu to her, and the dying flowers hung again on their stalks. So Mina went out of the field, and came again into the green lane. And here also everything seemed parched up with drought; the grass was burned down to a sort of hay along the dusty road-side, and the tall trees were almost yellow and faded for lack of wholesome moisture.

"Are you also thirsty?" asked Mina. "Poor pretty Trees, you look hot and tired."

"Give us rain, rain, rain!" whispered the Trees in a melodious rustle; "the green sap, the life-blood of our veins, is ebbing fast; give us rain or we shall die. Our leafy fingers have no strength left to play with the frolicsome breezes; we are perishing for want of water!"

"I am very sorry for you," said Mina, kindly, "but perhaps the nice dews will come to you by and bye, and then you will be refreshed again."

"If you were dying for want of water, under a scorching sun and a blazing sky, little maiden," answered a graceful Birch-tree, bending his feathery branches over her long curls; "do you think your thirst would be quenched with a few scanty drops of cool dew?"

Mina did not quite know what to say; so she waved a kindly adieu to the Trees and passed on, till she came to a broad grey stone, with a little hollow in it. A tall bramble grew close by; and on one of its long sprays sat a little robin, looking puffy and disconsolate.

"Pretty little Bob," said Mina, "how are you? I am so glad to see you!"

"I am *so* thirsty," said Robin; "my throat is so dry and parched, I can hardly breathe. And our own little pool here is empty; my brothers and kindred have all been here, hoping to find a drop or two, but it is in vain. I am so weak and faint, I have stayed here to rest till the evening, when I hope a little dew will fall and make the dusty grass damp."

Mina was very sorry for the poor little bird; but she could only give him pitying words.

"I will go and look in that green hollow yonder," said she; "the cows and horses are all there, and I dare say there is some water to be found. If I can get any, I will bring you some in a great dock-leaf."

Bob chirped forth his feeble thanks, and Mina set out on her kind errand. But when she reached the place, she found nothing but black mud, in which the cows were standing,—a wretched substitute for the cool clear water,—but still better than nothing. The poor cows looked warm and uncomfortable, and so did a couple of horses who were standing under a shady tree hard by.

"Is there no water anywhere near?" inquired Mina, timidly, of a handsome speckled Alderney, who was whisking incessantly with her tail, to keep off the flies.

"Water, indeed," answered the cow crossly; "no, we should have none to give away if there were any. That horrid Sun has dried up our pond even; and when it will ever rain again, goodness only knows, for there is not a cloud to be seen in the sky."

Mina was rather afraid of the cows, and horses, for they kicked up their heels quite viciously, and flourished their tails so fiercely at the flies, she was not sorry to get out of their neighbourhood. She then wandered on for a long distance, till she came to the place where a brooklet had been; but its course was now only marked by the rushes that had bordered it, and the water-cresses that grew in it. A few drops of sandy water still lay in a deep hole.

"Yes, my dear," it said "this is all that is left of the pretty little brook, that gleamed so brightly in the rays of the sun, and tinkled so merrily over the pebbles. There has been no rain, so that the springs that fed me have failed, and I am now only a ghost of myself."

"I am so sorry for you," said Mina. "And have you lost all your pretty forget-me-nots and cuckoo flowers?"

"Yes, quite," replied the Brook; but then, they have roots and seeds, that lie in the earth, and will spring up again another year. But oh! my poor little fishes, and merry tadpoles, they are all dead! I have not even a caddis-worm left. Every night, the stars hunt about for me among the long grass, and wonder what has become of their old friend."

Mina gossipped a good while with the Brook, and obtained from him a thimbleful of water for the poor Robin, who was thankful enough for the precious drops. Then Mina wandered on again, and presently she came to the outskirts of the village, and found herself beside the mill. But the great wheel stood idle, and the door was closed, although a group of children stood waiting round.

"What is the matter?" asked Mina, "are you waiting for any one?"

"We are waiting for what we can't have, Miss," replied one; "the miller has our wheat to grind, and he can't do it, because the stream is run dry for want of rain."

"We tan't have our take till de wain tumth!" lisped a chubby little girl, looking very dismal.

"And poor baby is ill, and wants his food so badly," murmured a tall girl at Mina's elbow.

"We worked so hard gleaning in the wheat-field," said Bobby Dobbs, "cos we thought we should have lots of bread; and mother promised us some dumplings!"

"How I wish we could see even a weeny little black cloud," said one.

"How nice it will be when the rain falls on the pavement!" cried another, "won't it smell sweet!"

"Oh lawk," said Bobby Dobbs, "won't it be

fun for the ducks; they are at their wit's ends for want of water. Our old drake tried so hard to bathe in a puddle, and poked down his head, and turned up his tail, and kicked wonderful, but there wasn't water enough to wet a feather of his wings."

"Mother gave Tommy such a beating yesterday," said Polly Trott, eager to tell her tale, "for sailing his boat in her milk-pans, cos he couldn't get no water nowheres!"

Mina burst out laughing at this recital of Tommy's troubles, and that broke the charm, and the vision fled. She found herself still snugly rolled up in the Siberian blanket, in the bay-window. When she had rubbed her eyes quite open, and collected her ideas, she pondered a little on all she had heard.

"I won't be such an ill-tempered, selfish little girl again," said she, "or wish for pleasure at other folk's expense. You dear little rain-drops, I am glad to see you now, chasing each other down the window-panes, for I know what good you are doing everywhere. How the poor thirsty poppies and corn must be revelling in the pleasant showers; and the trees stretching out their green hands, to be washed from dust by the cool rain. How fresh everything will look; and how nice everything will smell! The cows and horses will be able to have such a deep bath now, they will get quite lively. The mill-wheel will spin round, oh! so merrily, and the poor children can all have their bread, cake, and dumplings. And as for Tommy Trott, he will be able to sail his boat in grand style by his mother's door. I shall go and draw a picture of them all on my slate, with the drake diving head foremost in the corner. After all, a rainy day need not be quite disagreeable. I will go and tell Nurse all about my funny dream."

And Mina danced away quite merrily, singing to herself an amended version of her song of the morning:—

> "Rain, rain, come again,
> Go another day to Spain!"

A MORNING SONG.

THE lark is singing her morning lay,
The mist on the woods is dim and grey,
The sun is seeking the fairest rose,
And buds and blossoms each hour unclose;
The brook is singing in merry glee,
And just abroad is the busy bee,
The faint flush dawns in the rosy skies:
Come, dearest sister! awake! arise!

Come to the fresh and scented air,
To the woods and fields; let us gather there
The kingcup yellow and cowslip sweet,
(Like the golden traces of fairy feet),
The faint primroses and violets blue,
That wake each morning, to drink the dew;
The blossoms have opened their dainty eyes:
Sister! dear sister! awake! arise!

The silken nets the gossamer weaves
Are waving free from the glossy leaves,
The dewdrops be-stud them with many a pearl,
Fit for the coronet of an earl;
But the sun will kiss them, and they will flee,
Ere the shadow reaches the old elm tree;
He is mounting fast in the bright blue skies:
Come, dearest sister! awake! arise!

Birds in the chestnuts are stirring now,
They twitter and chirp upon every bough;
The lamb is awake, he has started away,
With the calves, and the little colt, to play;
The whole air rings with the joyous mirth
Of the young things dwelling on this green earth;
The sun climbs high in the far blue skies:
Come, dearest sister! awake! arise!

THE VOYAGE OF A LITTLE BOAT.

IDA and Otho were sister and brother, and they lived alone together in a grotto, by the shore of the great ocean. They did not remember any days in their lives, when they had not dwelt in their sheltering cave, so close by the murmuring tide; and the time passed on so pleasantly, that they scarcely noticed its flight. They loved each other very dearly, and were seldom far apart; so that whenever you saw Otho, you might be sure Ida was somewhere close at hand. Their clear young voices, harmonized and blended into the sweetest music, floating at evening so merrily over the waves, that the very winds seemed to be hushed and listening. A strip of silver sand stretched before the door of the cave, on which the sea, even in its very roughest moods, never encroached, save to waft rare shells and tangled weeds there for Ida to gather. And their lives were as peaceful and happy as a summer-day. Otho caught fish, and snared birds and rabbits, and such-like small deer, to supply their frugal fare; which Ida prepared with the herbs and roots, that grew plentifully on the green shore behind them.

One day, Otho, who had been wandering along the shore to watch his fishing-lines, ran suddenly home to his sister.

"Ida," he exclaimed, "I have found a treasure! I was sauntering up the little creek where we always go to look for clams, when I saw something lying by the edge of the shore, and when I came up to it, I found it was a boat!—a real boat!—big enough to hold us both!"

Ida clasped her hands with delight, and, proposed to set off for a voyage at once, as the day was fair, and the sea was calm.

"But we must have some provisions to take

with us," suggested Otho; "let us see what we have in our stores."

So they went to their larder, which was an opening or smaller cave, close by in the same rock. Here they took some bunches of dried grapes, some roots, some shells filled with wild honey, and some sea-bird's eggs, which Ida roasted in the ashes. Otho filled some skins with clear fresh water, and packed up some dried fish, so that they had ample stores for their journey. They loaded themselves with their provisions, and set off on their travels. Guided by Otho, Ida's quick eyes soon discerned the little boat, and she exclaimed in rapture, that it was fit for the queen of the fairies. It was painted of a rich dark brown outside, like a polished sea-shell, and lined with the tinted silvery hues of the mother-of-pearl within. It was shaped like the graceful nautilus, and had a sail of the thinnest and whitest stuff possible. Ida seated herself in the stern, and Otho cast loose the cable which moored them to the shore, formed of a single stem of the huge sea-weed, that arises from its roots many fathoms deep in the silent waters of the great Pacific.

"Whither shall we direct our course?" said Otho. "If it was dark and we could see the stars, those silver lamps of the night would guide us on our way."

"Let us trust to the wind," replied Ida; "there is a fresh breeze arising, let us be content to go whithersoever it will carry us."

And the little boat sailed on, and on—past lovely green islands adorned with feathery palm-trees; past low green shores, guarded by coral reefs; past rocky mountains, whose bases were washed by huge breakers. Still the little boat sailed on, without stop or stay, till it neared an island, which loomed dark and steep out of the sea, and whose summit seemed hid in the vapours of air, while its foot was obscured by the mists of ocean. Great waves rolled with a never-ceasing roar on its rock-bound sides, and endeavoured fruitlessly to creep up them, falling back in disappointed masses of angry foam. The little boat glided at a respectful distance round the island, till they came to an opening between the rocks, through which, after poising for a moment like a bird on the wing, it darted, with a swift silent rush, like the swoop of the falcon. When Otho and Ida recovered their senses, somewhat upset by the swiftness of their passage, and were able to shake off the blinding spray which had covered them, they found they were in a spacious land-locked bay, almost large enough for an inland lake, that lay in the centre of the rocky island walls.

They then found their little shallop was not the only one in those still waters, for they seemed to teem with craft of all sizes and sorts, quite motionless, yet with their sails set. There were huge vessels of war, armed and defended; elegant galleys, with gilded prows and silken awnings; and huge tub-like boats, that seemed heavily laden down to the water's edge. But what surprised them most of all was, the utterly motionless silence in which they all lay, so as to seem more like the painted images of some master hand than anything real. Not a ripple broke the surface of that quiet water; not a wave showed its white crest on that clear mirror.

"How I wish we had brought a pilot or guide, Ida," cried Otho; "I can't think where we are, nor can I see any one to ask."

Now they had observed, before setting sail, that the figure-head of their little boat was a very curious one. It had the fair, the very fair, face of a lovely woman, with deep tender eyes, and flowing wavy hair, that rippled over a long swan-like neck. But from the snowy shoulders grew radiant wings, which, although they were now furled, held the promise of glorious tints and hues, in their folded plumage. Round her slender waist was a girdle, which flashed and glittered with a deep red radiance, like a glowing fire; while below it, instead of fair shapely limbs, a glittering fish's-tail flowed in scaly bends and undulations.

When Otho uttered the wish, the fair figur e

turned her graceful head, and spoke to him, in the sweetest voice in the world.

"Those who are permitted to sail in my barque, need not guide or pilot. Those who seek me, and listen to my voice, can gain all they wish to know."

Then Otho and Ida fearfully entreated the fair shape to sit with them in the boat; but she told them she could not leave her post, for if she did, the little boat would instantly become a prey to the wind and waves. She spoke in the most melodious voice they had ever heard; so they both hung entranced on her words, while they asked her questions, as much for the sake of the music of her words, as for the knowledge they contained.

"This is the Bay of the Lost Hopes!" said she. "Here lie the ships that never come home. Do you see that stately vessel yonder? she is freighted with ingots of gold from stem to stern; and her owner, a merchant, has looked for her, day after day, for years, and will do so while he lives. Yonder little barque carries dresses, toys, sweetmeats, for the merry children of a loving mother; but they have long been in the churchyard, and their mother does not wish to see her ship come home, for she would have no use for its cargo. Yonder vessel is laden with pictures, carvings, and works of art; but its owners have long ago ceased to care for it; they look for other sorts of merchandise now. If I could open all the holds of those motionless ships, you would see curious hoards of treasures there, mostly gold and jewels; but sometimes better things. And the reason the bay is not more crowded than it is, is because when the owners die, the ships sink, —down, like a stone, they go, with all their cargo, without leaving a ripple on the glassy waters. See, there goes one even now before our eyes!"

And Otho and Ida beheld a little graceful shallop, fluted like a sea-shell, and painted with the loveliest hues within and without. Gold tipped her spars and oars, like rays of sun-shine; and flags of the brightest hues floated from her masts. Down she went sinking, sinking; first her carved and gilded hull; then the snowy spreading sails; the slender tapering masts; the filmy silken ropes; one moment, and the azure pennon at her mast-head, was gone utterly and silently, disappearing like the red sun when he dips into the sea, and goes suddenly out of our sight to light another part of the world. Otho and Ida drew a deep, long sigh, and looked an each other somewhat sadly.

"And now," said the fair creature who had told them this, "let me take you on a more cheerful expedition. Close your eyes, and hold fast, for my boat travels other ways than by the sea."

Thus saying, she furled the snowy sail at a touch; and Otho and Ida, with closed eyes and shortened breath, felt themselves sinking, sinking, like the vessel they had watched, till with a shudder, like that of a living being, the boat stood fast. They opened their eyes fearfully, and gazed about them, half blinded by the mingled glare and darkness that broke on their astonished sight. They seemed to be down fathoms below the earth, and instead of sailing on cool, clear, green water, they seemed to be wafted on waves of liquid flame.

"This is the Fire-world," said the fair shape who was their guide, and who still stood at the prow of the vessel. The fiery red light lit up her bright eyes and golden hair, and sparkled with a lurid splendour on the glowing girdle round her slender waist. Ida shrank closer to her brother, and clasped her trembling arms round him, for she was afraid of this awfully-grand Fire-world; but Otho was too proud to show his fear, so he only held his sister very tightly, and did not speak. The boat still kept sailing on over the waves, which glistened with a pale bluish light, as you may often see the sea-waves do on a dark night, except that these were far more brilliant. And presently they beheld tall towers and battlements from out of the fiery sea; and splendid domes and palaces; which all melted, as it were, and grew into other shapes so fast, that Otho and Ida could hardly remember them.

"These are the buildings you see in the fire at evening!" said their guide; "all those graceful palaces and airy spires, that you have traced so often, are built down here. And sometimes they take shape in other ways, and are made permanent joys and beauties for ever. Many a poet, painter, or architect, has, while brooding over his lonely fire at night, half-unconsciously drunk into his soul the forms and fashions of grace and loveliness, that have inspired him with the creations of genius. For in earth, air, fire or water, all is order and harmony, even when it seems in greatest confusion; and human Art is but the hand-maid and follower of divine Nature,—borrowing copies from her unstudied perfection, which is always good, in whatever form it shows itself. Now the Fire-artists are very wonderful in their way; and most impartial, like the Sun, they often save their finest performances for the lowliest subjects. The lights and shadows they send from the wide glowing hearth of the fisherman's cottage, are generally more worthy of the painter's skill, than the prisoned heat of the costly polished stove, that warms the saloons of the wealthy. Indeed, I may say the Fire-world is peculiarly the heritage of the poor, the third necessary of existence after food and drink. But it is time we were going farther: we are going to pass out of the Fire-country to another land."

Then the little boat began to ascend again; and Otho and Ida closed their eyes as before, to escape seeing the perils of the way. When they opened them again, they were sailing down a long canal, whose end they could not discover, for it wound along in a devious course, and its banks were fringed by tall trees and bushes. The path that skirted the side of the water, was closely paved with little three-cornered gray stones, with inscriptions in small letters on each one; and this pavement seemed to stretch on for miles, as if it had no end.

"This is the road that is paved with Good Intentions," said the fair shape. "When mortals make plans and resolves that are good and right, and perform them, they lay stones to build up their houses with; but when they only *think* good resolutions, and are too weak or indolent to carry them into effect, they are adding so many blocks to pave this road with; which is already so long, that even *I* do not know the end of it!"

Presently a low ridge of rock appeared by the side of the water, which rose abruptly, till it formed itself into a vast natural mass of stone, apparently hollowed into a cave, to which admission was given by a narrow door in the rock.

Hand in hand, in obedience to their guide, Otho and Ida entered the dark aperture. For an instant they could scarcely see in the dim light of the interior, coming as they did from the full blaze of sunshine. But when their eyes were somewhat more accustomed to it, they discerned in one corner an old woman, with flowing grey hair, and keen bright eyes, in a strange white gown, who was busily engaged in spinning at a wheel that stood before her. Round went the wheel, and away sped the glistening threads, dark, bright, and many-coloured, as they were dexterously twisted by the lean fingers of the aged woman; now gleaming with gold and silver, or the borrowed hue and lustre of the most precious gems, and then black and dull, and of the coarsest fibre. But the old woman seemed regardless of their changes, and did not lift her head even when Otho and Ida stood close beside her. They watched her for some time, and then Ida asked her timidly, in her sweet low voice, what she was doing.

"I am spinning stories," replied the old woman; "tales of travel, fairie land, and science; stories of wonderful adventures and gallant deeds; histories, true and false, comic or sad. You see the variegated hues of my threads as they go; but it is all alike to me, for the years pass on, and I am still kept spinning! spinning! spinning! The woolly stuff you see yonder is made of the brains of authors; and according as they were merry or sad, so are the threads of my work. But it is weary work;

for centuries past, I have been weary, but I am obliged to go on, spinning! spinning! spinning!"

Ida laid her soft hand kindly on the old woman's arm; but she had turned to her work again, and dropped her dull eyes on the bright-hued threads that, at the moment, flowed under her withered fingers. So Ida and Otho turned away, and, in the other corner, they beheld a man turning a grindstone, from which flew brilliant sparks at every turn. The man was gaunt and thin, and his bones and muscles stood up like great cords on his lean arms. His face was hollow and pale; his lips compressed and stern, as he laboured ceaselessly at the huge stone wheel. He was clothed in thin rags, which fluttered uneasily at every movement, and at the keen wind which blew in through the door. He paused from his toil, and lifted his bright eyes to gaze for a moment upon the youthful pair before him, while a faint smile, like a wintry sunbeam, flickered over his wan features.

"What are you grinding?" enquired Otho, encouraged by his kindly expression.

"Bright thoughts, and noble ideas!" replied the lean man, very softly, in a low, sweet voice. "Each spark that flies from my wheel is some grand song to benefit suffering humanity, some psalm of life, to encourage earth's pilgrims on their way. Not easily or lightly are they created, for slight means cannot move this ponderous wheel; but ground out with many a painful revolution—many a day of suffering, and night of toil. Bright sparks are they, with hearts of fire, that seek out and illumine the dark spots of earth, and do their appointed work, even if it be only for a little space."

"Are you not weary?" asked Ida, gently. "Your companion seems to long for rest; do you not need it also?"

"Very weary!" answered the pale man, with a low sigh; "but there is a rest coming to all! And now I cannot pause to speak with you, for my work must go on, on, never ceasing; my wheel must be ever turning."

Then Otho and Ida departed slowly from this wonderful earth-cavern, and stood once more in the pleasant sunshine, by the side of their little boat. Then, from its sides, at the bidding and touch of the fair figure at the prow, sprouted four delicate, bat-like, wings, on which it mounted, buoyant as a bird, into the sunny realms of air, but going far higher, than even the kingly eagle, with his vast and sinewy pinions, would dare to soar.

"This is the most charming sailing of all!" said Ida, delighted, and clapping her little hands with glee. "See, dear Otho, how the boat goes through the air, as swiftly and steadily as she did through the water; and the fleecy clouds are our foaming waves, now!"

And they passed through the store-house of all the clouds, where they lay piled up ready for use — golden, and crimson, and delicate violet. And their beautiful guide smiled sweetly on Ida, and asked her how she would like to live in Cloudland.

"Oh, so much!" replied Ida, eagerly; "so

very much. It must be such a lovely thing, to sail about on this sea of clouds, or stop, now and then, at some of those shining star islands!"

And presently they came to a broad cloud-meadow, on each side of which rose fine castles and battlemented towers, that seemed built of the moon-beams, they were so bright and so shining. They were far more beautiful than the buildings of the Fire-world, for they were so light and aërial, and tinged with delicate hues, like the bubbles that children blow.

"These are the castles in the air, which people build, but never inhabit, for they would not bear the touch of a finger; and, shining and lovely as they seem, they are for ever tenantless, Ida; and fade away with the thoughts of their mortal architects."

Ida watched one fairy structure, rich with airy domes and delicate spires, and set with wrought pinnacles and graceful tracery; and she saw it fading away, slowly, slowly, as the rainbow does in the heavens, till it leaves nothing but the blue, bright sky behind it.

Then the little boat once more expanded its bat-like wings fully, and sailed off on its downward way. And it went down a broad, golden path to the earth again, passing the lovely, fleecy clouds on its track, which were lit up with the brightest violet hues by the rays of the setting sun. And Ida noticed thousands of little, bright atoms floating about, and spinning merrily in the golden stream they were sailing down. The fair shape told her, these were the little dust-motes that were always dwelling in the beautiful sun-rays, as they come sliding down to the earth. When they came to the end of their sunbeam track, they found they had reached the green hillock that lay behind their cave.

"And now," said the fair shape, "I must bid you farewell; for I have so much to do I can stay no longer with you."

Ida and Otho thanked her warmly and often for their charming voyage, and took a sorrowful leave of the beautiful little vessel which had borne them so safely and so pleasantly.

"You will think of us often," said the graceful shape, "in your pleasant home by the sea; and, perhaps, some day, my little boat may come for you again. Meanwhile, be as happy and loving as you have hitherto been; and you will never lack friends or enjoyment. I do not think you will soon forget the wanderings you have had, or the voyage you made, with Fancy for your guide, and a Dream for your boat, through the enchanted realms of Vision-land, the Fire-world, and the Cloud-region!"

WHAT THE DAISY SAID TO THE LARK.

A PRETTY little Daisy grew on a wide common. There were plenty of flowers of all sorts growing near; for was there not the yellow Gorse, with its golden honey-scented blossoms; and the purple Heath, with its delicate bells; besides Foxgloves, and Harebells, and Ferns, and many more pleasant people whom I have no time to mention? But, strangely enough, it chanced that there was but one Daisy to be seen far or near. Perhaps it was because wise old mother Nature knew that there were other flowers and plants, enough and to spare, for bee and bird, and for all other wandering children of hers as well; so that she reserved her Daisies for the blank corners, and bare churchyards of the great city, places that needed them far more.

There was a Lark who lived hard by. She had made her nest in a pretty hollow, covered with the creeping, sweet-scented wild Thyme, and sheltered by a noble Gorse-bush. There she had woven her little home of slender bents, lined carefully with soft grass; and there were her five pretty grey eggs tended, watched, and kept warm. One day, to her great joy, while she was resting there, she espied, quite close to her, the fair little Daisy, looking up with its innocent white face and golden eye, from its flat green leaves.

"Dear friend," cried the Lark, "(for your family and mine have always been friends from the early beginning), how is it we never met before?"

"We often pass over things that lie near home," said the Daisy, smiling; "but I am only a late visitor, for I have not been here very long, so no wonder you never spied me before."

THE DAISY AND THE LARK.

Page 166.

"Pray how came you here?" inquired the Lark, quite rejoiced to have a friendly chat.

"I have travelled a long way," answered the Daisy, and perhaps the history of some of my wanderings will interest you."

The Lark, quite delighted, eagerly begged her to proceed; and settled herself down cosily over her eggs to listen to the story.

"My last home," said the Daisy, "was in a dark corner, in a small close alley, in a great town. I can hardly describe, and you would scarcely credit, the horrible state of the place. The dark dirty houses soared up high and black, as if trying for a glimpse of the blue sky, which their inhabitants never obtained there. The pavement below was full of holes, which contained dark pools of filthy liquid, the washings from sooty roofs, and still dirtier floors. Every window was glazed with a film of dust and smoke, till the original glass, cracked and broken as it was, could scarcely be seen. The insides of these miserable dens must have matched their outer appearance; but of these I only heard. I grew in a little scrap of earth, about the size of an ant's nest, that chanced to be in one corner: and I tried to keep my green leaves and little flower-buds as clean as I could. But, after all, what could they be but dingy stunted things, fed on such wretched fare, and washed only in such polluted streams.

"One day a little child crawled out of one of the dens near, for I cannot call them homes. She was like one of my own poor little buds; for the childish beauty, that would have brightened her little face in a more wholesome atmosphere, was here withered and dwarfed to precocious age. Her blue eyes looked unnaturally large from the thin face, where every bone almost was sharply defined under the sallow unhealthy skin.

"'Pretty little thing,' she muttered to herself, when she saw me, 'what are you? a feather of a white bird, or a flake of snow?'

"'I am a friend, little one,' I answered softly; 'a poor one it is true, and not able to help you. But I can tell you stories, and whisper pleasant things to you.'

"Then her poor pale blue eyes were as near

being bright as they could be, and she clapped her small bony hands.

"'Dear little thing,' she said, 'I don't know your name, or what you are, so I shall call you my Comfort. I heard mother say once before she died, that she had one "*Great* Comfort," and it seemed to make her so happy, it must have been something nice. So I shall call you my 'Little Comfort,' and come and see you every day.'

"And the tiny creature kept her promise; and crawled out day after day to the low corner where I grew. And every bit of cheer and consolation that I could think of, did I pour, as well as I could, into the little withered heart. I murmured stories of the pleasant green fields, where the young lambs lie so cosily nestled up by the side of the old sheep, and the buttercups spread a sheet of gold for the sleek cows to feed on. And I tried to recollect some of the sayings of one of your family, a Lark I used to know once, who had flown up into the clear blue sky, and seen the stars shining so brightly.

" 'I see the stars, too, sometimes,' said the little child, 'and they look so kind and gentle; but oh! so far, far off.'

" Then I told her of all the flowers that grew in the hedges and lanes; the roses and honey-suckles, and the graceful meadow-sweet.

" 'I have seen flowers, too, in the shop-windows in the streets,' said she, 'but I never touched one, though I should like it, they look so soft and bright.'

"Poor little one! she ought to have lived among flowers and birds, for she was a tender, gentle-hearted little creature; and she was dying fast in the unwholesome air of that wretched den. Day after day the dull eyes grew more sunken, and the little lips more white; while the feeble feet tottered more and more, as she crept about the dirty pavement, or sat idly playing with a few oyster-shells, her only toys. Many a bitter blow and rough push did she receive from the wretched, wicked people she lived among, but she took it all very patiently. At last, one day, the cruel woman with whom she dwelt, and who grudged her every mouldy crust she gave her, scolded her fiercely for letting the few damp sticks, which she had put up for a fire, burn out; and, after giving her some rough shakes, she snatched me up angrily from the corner and flung me over the wall into the street. I heard one piteous cry of, 'Oh, my Comfort! my poor little Comfort! Don't take it away from me.' And that was the last I knew of my dear little child-friend; except that, after I was cast out of the alley, I fell on the ledge of a wall in the outer street, and I soon after saw a little, roughly knocked-up coffin of bare boards, carried out on the parish bier, and trotted off to the burying-ground—alone—but not more lonely than the child had been in her sorrowful, neglected, short life. There was no pall or covering over the miserable coffin, but I shed down two or three withered leaves and buds upon it. I could not regret her; for did I not know that the stunted, withered little heart, that had never known a joy or a pleasure, was now expanding in the brighter light of another sun?

"In fact, I have only one regret," continued the Daisy, with tears in her pink eyes; "I am only grieved that perverse fate brought me here, and that I was not permitted to grow and blossom over her grave."

"Dear friend," said the Lark, "there are many, many such perishing little ones in our great towns — children without a play-ground, without toys, without flowers; and our only consolation, insufficient as it is, is, that though man neglects and despises them, the great Father of all loves and cares for them, and Heaven has in store for them the joys and blessings they were denied here!"

"And this is the end of my story," said the Daisy.

LITTLE PRINCESS MARJORIE.

THERE was a Queen in the West
    countrie,
  She had one little daughter, fair to
    see;
Her eyes were like stars, and her locks of gold,
In waving curls, to her small feet rolled.
    Fair, fair, passing fair,
    With her locks of golden hair,
    Was little Princess Marjorie!

The Queen she combed them, at morn and eve,
And thick in the tresses white pearls did weave;
She plaited red gold, she twined-in the gem,
Till the little head grew weary of them.
    Fair, fair, passing fair,
    Those heavy braids of jewelled hair,
    Of little Princess Marjorie!

They clad her fine, in satin and silk,
Red as the ruby, and white as the milk,
With sandals of silver, and girdle of gold,
And each tress gleamed brightly as down it rolled.
Fair, fair, stately fair,
With robe, and crown, and plaited hair,
Was little Princess Marjorie!

She looked at the daisies that bloomed on the lea,—
"I wish," she sighed, "that they grew for me;
I'd give all the white pearls set in my hair;
For a daisy chain round my neck to wear."
Fair, fair, very fair,
With her pensive, childish air,
Was this little Marjorie!

This tender Princess grew sick and thin,
The roses faded from her white skin;
Her footsteps faltered, she hung down her head,
And turned from the banquet before her spread.
Fair, fair, passing fair,
With those clouds of golden hair,
Was little Princess Marjorie!

The Queen, in terror, sent for the leech;
He came at her call, and made a long speech;
He gazed at the child, as she lay in bed;
He twiddled his fingers, and shook his head.
Fair, fair, still so fair,
Pillowed lay the golden hair
Of pale little Marjorie!

Then up rose old Nurse, as she sat by,
A frown on her brow, and a tear in her eye;
"Away with your fashions! just give her to me,
She was well enough when she played by my knee.
Fair, fair, well and fair,
A little maid with golden hair,
Was happy Princess Marjorie!

"Take off the silk robe, and the satin gown,
The weight of their folds is wearing her down;
Let her don a white kirtle, fair and free,
And away to the heath-clad hills with me.
Fair, fair, more than fair,
With rosy cheeks and tangled hair,
I'll bring back little Marjorie!

"Pull off the brooch, and the heavy gem,
You weighed all her young life down with them;
With chains of silver, and links of gold,
You made her life-blood run dull and cold.
Fair, fair, sadly fair,
With fettered locks of jewelled hair,
Poor little Princess Marjorie!

"I'll spin her a robe, of russet hue,
That can take no harm from sun or dew;
The brook shall sparkle, the free wind blow
A healthy kiss on the open brow.
Fair, fair, fresh and fair,
With her curls of sunny hair,
She'll be merry little Marjorie!

"A crown of flowers lies soft and light
Among my darling's tresses bright;
She'll mate with the birds, be friends with the bee,
Her throne green moss, and her court the lea!
Fair, fair, more than fair,
Rich in sunshine and free air,
Will then be our little Marjorie!"

THE STORY OF THE PAINTED WINDOW.

MY Lady Blanche was a great heiress. She lived in a grand old house, that was grey with age, in the midst of a large park, shaded with fine old trees, whose sap had flowed through the green shoots of many springs, and the golden faded leaves of many autumns. Dappled deer grazed quietly and safely among the thick fern, and sported, with their pretty little fawns, across the sunny glades.

I dare say I hear you say, what a very happy person Lady Blanche must have been! Young and beautiful, with great riches, and broad acres of forest and moorland, and this splendid home to live in, all her own! But you are wrong;

for it is not gold and silver, fine houses or broad lands that make people happy. There is a great deal wanted besides this, and quite apart from it, to make life at all a pleasant thing; and very often you may see smiling faces and loving hearts in a low dark room, that has nothing else to gild and brighten it up; while sorrow and death can make even a great palace lonely and desolate. Lady Blanche had every blessing in the world, except near and dear relations. She had been an only child, and her parents died when she was very young. She had known a great deal of sorrow in her long life, for she was now an aged woman, with no kind brothers to care for her, nor little children to love her. She dressed in the richest silks and velvets, and wore chains and bracelets of gold on her withered neck and arms; but it was from custom now, and not from any pride in them; for there were no loving eyes to look at her. And when she ate her dinner, it was from silver or gold; but the little sparrow, who perched under her window, feasted as well as she did, though he only ate grubs and seeds, and drank from the hollow of a leaf; but he had his merry little mate beside him, and a nestful of eggs into the bargain. I dare say Lady Blanche would have been pleased enough to hear the merry patter of little feet on her polished oaken floors, and the silvery sounds of children's laughter, ringing through the great empty house.

It was a beautiful mansion, where everything was set in such exact order, that the very dust seemed to be afraid to settle there. But the finest room in the house was my Lady's own chamber. The lofty ceiling was painted to represent a sky at night, with soft fleecy clouds, and here and there a star shining through. Then there was a grand old chimney-piece, carved with garlands of flowers, and piles of fruit. They looked so natural, it seemed as if they were only waiting for a troop of merry children to come and gather them. There were roses and lilies, with their buds and leaves; and round apples, and bunches of grapes, with their graceful tendril-rings and foliage; but spring and autumn brought no change or harvest to them.

The walls were hung with curious old-fashioned paper, which had once been thought the very perfection of art and skill. Staring shepherdesses, in hoops and flower-sprinkled hats, with knots of ribbon on their crooks, sat under shady trees; and smart shepherds, in stiff-curled wigs, and ruffles, leant cross-legged against the gates, and played on their pipes; while their lambs, all bearing a strong family-likeness to each other, were feeding about. The furniture that was in the room was all in perfect keeping with it; gilded cabinets from Japan, held unknown treasures of foreign shells and curiosities. Dark carved ebony tables, with thin spiral spider-legs, supported delicate transparent china, and baskets and boxes, made in lands far beyond the sea. Huge chairs stood round the room, with square straight backs, their seats being covered with ancient silver brocade, the relics of some by-gone court-train.

At one end of the room was a noble painted window, that threw its rich hues, on sunny days, on the polished oaken floor. This painted window was the very pride of Lady Blanche's heart. It was round, and divided into narrowing divisions, that met in the centre like the rays of the daisy petals. And in each compartment was painted the shield, or coat of arms, of some royal or noble family, from whom Lady Blanche was descended, and of whom she was now the sole and last representative. There gleamed the royal rose, and the Scottish lions; the scallop-shell, the proud emblem of the crusader, and the red hand was all over the window. To those who could read the language of Heraldry by her picture-writing, there was many a chronicle of noble deeds and hard-won honours. These richly-coloured panes were set in the luxuriant tracery of a delicately-carved stone frame.

Outside this window, in the garden below, grew an ancient rose-tree, which had sprung up and flourished through many generations, and become knotted and gnarled through age, like an old apple-tree. Now this rose-tree had for years wanted to be friendly with the great grand window near which she grew, and could not understand why he would not receive her advances. She had softly caressed him with her green leaves, and sportively tapped him with her little buds, laying her soft white face tenderly against him; but all in vain. He would never take the least notice of her, so that she shed great tears of dew at his haughty behaviour.

"You have glowing smiles for all the insensible things in that dull room," sighed the Rose; "but I can never win you to cast your glorious hues on my white leaves!"

"No," replied the Window, in a harsh, creaking voice, "I have nothing to do with you. Do you not belong to the outer world of common things, in which I am not concerned? I have no interest for any but my own people, for they only are worthy of it. I can crown the shepherd yonder with my golden lustre, and visit the cheek of the shepherdess with a crimson blush; while I can also light up the carved garlands into vivid green or tender blue, till they glow like the jewelled fruit of the fairies. But with your common every-day world I can hold no intercourse; vulgar things that live on dew and sunshine are no mates for me. I shine with the blazoned honours of a race of kings and nobles, so I can't stoop to your acquaintance!"

Then the Rose drew up her fair white head proudly, and said: "I, too, have my honours; and I do not consider myself so much your inferior. Has not every bride of your lordly house, borne my snowy blossoms in her shining hair on her wedding day? And no coffin lies in the family vault in yonder church, that does not enclose some of my withered leaves, laid on the cold breast, and dropping from the folded hands. But, after all, if *you* despise me, the dews and the winds love me and serve me!"

"I don't care for your dews and winds," said the Window, churlishly; "let them fall or blow if they like. I take no heed of such things."

Then he was so put out with the remarks of the Rose, that he did a great many disagreeable things. For instance, he gave the poor shepherdess a frightful red nose and green hair, and bestowed a bright yellow hue on the whole face of the shepherd; while he blotted the lambs all over black patches, till they looked like pigs.

Now the zephyrs had been fluttering about among the myrtle leaves, and they overheard the argument between the Rose and the Window; and the contemptuous way in which the latter spoke of their ruler and relative, the Wind. So as it happened that nothing delighted them more than a bit of gossip, off they went, carrying the whole report, much exaggerated after the manner of tale-bearers, to the ears of the Wind. And the Wind was in a terrible rage just then, for his ally, the Sea, had called him in, to help him in an onslaught on a lighthouse, that stood on a bare rock, far from the shore. The Wind and the Sea, by their united power, had already blown down and washed away several wooden lighthouses that had been erected there. But, since then, some persevering man had built one of stone, and so strongly, too, that it defied the utmost power of the allied forces. And the Wind had come back in a very bad temper, and he was by no means pleased with the story the Zephyrs brought him. Accordingly, without more ado, he rushed off to the spot, and blew the huge limb of a giant oak tree quite through the painted window, and sent its many-coloured panes down in shivered fragments on the ground beneath. Then the Rose, mourning over the untimely end of her ungracious neighbour, cast her white-scented petals over his shattered remains.

Lady Blanche was so sorely grieved for the destruction of her beautiful window, that she vowed it should not be replaced by another, which would only remind her of the loss. So the stone tracery was filled up with plain white glass, and the shepherds and shepherdesses were obliged to be content with their own faded charms, and forego the deep ruby and glowing golden tints, that had formerly so often adorned them.

The Lady Blanche had taken into her service an aged gardener, who had now lived with her for several years. In his youth he had travelled in many countries, and gathered a vast store of varied knowledge. In no other gardens did the flowers thrive so well, and nowhere else could you see such skilful combinations of rich colours, as in the flower-beds of this stately old garden. But he knew the secret of many things as well as flowers, and was the wise man of the country round in particular. He had one little grandchild, the only creature that belonged to him, whom he watched and cherished with the tenderest care. She learnt all that she knew from his lips, during the quiet winter evenings, after his work was done; and was far better instructed than many children twice her age. She was quite learned in the histories and habits of bees, butterflies, and birds; and could tell every leaf at sight. She had quite a collection of treasures, which her grandfather had gathered for her: dried mosses and ferns; curious nests, and birds' eggs; indeed he seldom came home without some little addition to her museum.

One evening, he came in and told her he had brought her a present that he thought would please her much; and it was something she had never seen before. Then he produced a long green tube, something like a small telescope, and told her to hold it up to the light, and peep through the little round hole at one end, turning it gently round as she did so.

"Grandfather, I can see colours! red and blue, like the Lady's bracelets; and gold like her chain. Oh, Grandfather—it moves!—Is it alive? What can it be? It is like a flower opening before my eyes, only brighter. Is it the workshop of the fairies, Grandfather, where they make all the flowers?"

The old man laughed at her notion, and explained to her that he had made it for her himself, and put into it some of the bright fragments of the beautiful old window, which he had carefully collected after the sad accident. There was some of the ruby red, that used to flush the shepherdesses' cheeks; and the emerald-green, and sapphire-blue, that had tinted the garlands of flowers and fruit on the old chimney-piece, so that it was now a pretty relic of the glories of the noble window.

"Oh thank you, dear Grandfather!," cried the delighted child; "I hardly know what it is most like—jewels or flowers. What a great treasure it will be to me; and will it not help us to arrange the flower-beds in the Lady's garden? Here is a pattern very like the border round the great fountain—ah it is gone, and a prettier still is come! It seems always changing to some new form. But still, through all its changes and differences, it is always like a rose, round and many-coloured, as if the colours of the great window had fallen down on a white rose, and been held fast there!"

HIGH LIFE BELOW STAIRS.

"WHAT a delightful thing life is!" observed the House-fly, as he settled on the kitchen-table, to taste a little drop of spilt beer. "Every want of mine is supplied in the easiest manner possible. Fine gilt frames, and spacious looking-glasses, are put up for me to walk upon; and when I am tired of them, I can settle on the choice nick-nacks which decorate my apartments. Nay, so far do human beings carry their attention to my comfort, that they even provide me with an elegant little bower, hung up in a sunny window, all trellis-work and coloured paper; and this is specially and entirely devoted to me alone, and prettily designated a 'fly-cage.' In fact, mortals seem to devote their whole lives to my welfare."

"You make a slight mistake!" remarked a Wasp, sarcastically, who had just crawled out of a half-empty pot of apricot-jam; "you make, what I may call indeed, a rather large mistake. You seem to forget there are other people in the world besides yourself. For instance, look at me! Now, I don't profess to be anything very great, but I cannot in conscience fail to perceive the vast amount of trouble that is taken to provide for myself and my family. What do men plant fruit-trees in such profusion and variety for, except that I may revel in apricots, plums, pears, and whatever other sorts of fruit I prefer? What do the female portion of the race devote whole days and weeks in preserving these delicious fruits for, but that they may serve as my winter store. Just imagine all the trouble they take for *me*, and then pray don't boast of the attention *you* receive!"

"There's not a pin to choose between you!" said a third speaker, a little Mouse, who had come out of her hole under the dresser, and was now trimming her whiskers, and listening with much amusement to their conversation. "What are a few rubbishing fruits and sweets after all? Just as trumpery as the flowers, for which *I* could never see any use in my life. You are a couple of foolish little creatures to imagine the world only made for yourselves. Now I have more reasons to flatter myself on that score; for look at the toil and trouble, the months of care and anxiety the human species bestow on their corn-fields, and all in order that my relations, and their friends, the birds, may live upon nice wheat and barley. As for myself, I need only point to the huge dairies of cows kept, whose entire produce is devoted to making cheese—delicious fat rich cheese; and for whom? Why, for Me!"

Then a little black Ant crawled up the leg of the kitchen-table, and loudly asserted his claim to the world and its pleasures. "See," said he, "how the slaves toil under a burning sun to grow and prepare sugar for *us*; besides treacle, and other little extra treats I need not mention. Why, in foreign parts, we are treated with immense respect; and the human two-legged creatures even sometimes vacate their houses when my brethren approach, besides packing up huge cases and parcels of sundry sorts, to appease our appetites when we take to travelling!"

At last the controversy grew loud and strong, each asserting his right to the best of everything; and boldly proclaiming the world was made for him, and for him alone. In fact, they made such a noise over it that the Blackbeetle came out of his hole under the copper, in the back-kitchen, for he thought the house was on fire at least. When he found out the cause of the riot, he laughed so he nearly tumbled over the broom-handle.

"Candles and cheese!" shrieked the mouse.

"Plum-jam, and currant-jelly!" buzzed the enraged Wasp, dancing angrily about.

"Sugar and treacle," squeaked the Ant, as he trotted here and there in his fury.

"Cornices and fly-cages," piped the Fly, who had perched himself on the mantel-piece, at a safe distance from the contending parties.

"Oh dear! oh dear!" ejaculated the Blackbeetle, as he propped himself up against the fender to rest, after laughing till he nearly cried; "what an amusing set of people you are! I have only one observation to add to yours, and that is, that *I* ought to claim the largest share of the world, for there are few things that come amiss to me—bread, meat, flour; everything eatable, in fact, was made for me, and me only!"

Then the Cricket poked his nose out of his hole under the oven, and laid his claim to all the milk, broth, and liquid food to be found. Then said the Blackbeetle:

"I don't see any use in all this quarrelling. Idle words and boasting don't fill folk's stomachs. I vote for a general adjournment of the question till this night week."

The Ant, who was very greedy and covetous, and had already scented some food, eagerly seconded the motion, which was eventually carried by unanimous consent. Then the Blackbeetle trotted off to ascertain the flavour of some new and delicious preparation, which he found put for him, (with a delicate remembrance of his peculiar habits,) close to his usual hole under the copper. The Mouse had before broken her fast on some crumbs of cake, that were scattered about, so she only amused herself for a time by nibbling a fresh door of communication to her hole in the wainscot. By and bye, feeling rather tired, she mounted the table again, and there she met the Fly.

"I can't think what's the matter with the Blackbeetle," he said; "he has been taken alarmingly ill,—so ill that Mrs. Beetle and her large young family were summoned to his assistance. They considered, however, he had, perhaps, partaken somewhat too largely of some fine red cakes that had been provided for him; so Mrs. Beetle was going to give him a warm bath, and I hope he will be better!"

"It's a fit of apoplexy, I dare say," replied the Mouse severely; "and he deserves it for his greediness. And do you know, a merited fate has overtaken that boasting, covetous Ant;

for I saw him as I passed, quite lifeless floating legs uppermost, in a large pond of some sweet liquid. So *he* at last has found out that the world was not quite made for *him!*"

Then the Mouse and the Fly set off together in search of the Cricket; but they hunted high and low, and could not find her.

"It's no great loss," remarked the Fly, "for really she had such a loud voice, she shook every nerve in my body!"

"I did not care so much about her voice," answered the Mouse; "but I do so hate practical jokes; and her absurd jumps and starts worried me to death!"

Then they abandoned their vain search, for she was not to be seen anywhere,—and no wonder, for she was lying at the bottom of the pan of milk, wherein she had drowned herself while she was drinking. On their way, however, they heard the Wasp shrieking for help, and they found him in a large round glass-house, kicking and struggling among a host of his dead and dying companions, who were all suffocated in a thick mixture of treacle and beer.

"Such is life!" observed the Mouse, with a sigh. "It is very sad to see our neighbours drop off in this way. Let us go and inquire how the Blackbeetle is!"

Then they went to his house, and knocked at the door, which was opened by one of his children, who showed them into the usual sitting-room of the family, where they beheld the dead Beetle laid out, with his widow sitting weeping at his head, and his little ones, two-and-two, at each side.

"Oh," groaned the disconsolate widow, "how lucky we had plenty of mourning! My poor dear departed! Those unwholesome wafers were doubtless the cause of his death!"

"Calm yourself, my dear creature," said the Mouse, soothingly; "as I remarked before, such is life! We have all our gains and our losses. Come, my friend, we must depart."

And, to keep up her spirits, the Mouse went off to seek something for lunch. She smelt a most exquisite perfume, and found it proceeded from a tempting slice of delicately-toasted cheese.

"Good creatures!" cried the Mouse, "how they have taken all this trouble for me; and have not only provided this dainty supper for me, but have laid it ready in a pretty little house, with an airy window. Really, my feelings almost overpower me—the sight of the unfortunate Blackbeetle's corpse has upset me so. I *must* take a morsel just to keep up my strength. As Dr. Twiddlewhisker truly observes, my delicate frame requires double the quantity of nourishment that stronger persons need. Adieu, my friend the Fly, perhaps we shall meet again ere long!"

Then the Mouse hastily trotted into the nice little place; and in the first hurry of her delicate appetite, and, perhaps, also from the shattered state of her nerves, she did not notice the slight circumstance, that the little door behind her had fallen down. By and bye, however, she was disturbed during her half-finished meal, by the tiny shrieks of the Fly, and she then discovered she was shut in; so she went and peeped out of the window.

"Help! help!" sighed the Fly, faintly; "I am caught—I am dying; come and help me, Mrs. Mouse, I beseech you!"

"I would with the greatest pleasure in life," called the Mouse, "but my friends who made this pretty house for me, have carelessly forgotten to put a latch to the door, and the wind has blown it to, so I must stop till they let me out. But what is the matter?"

"Alas!" sighed the Fly, growing weaker and weaker, "I only walked up this lovely glazed surface, that looked so smooth and soft, and was so sweet and nice, and my poor wings stuck to it so fast, that I nearly dislocated my shoulder in my efforts to get away; and now I am so worn out with struggling, my legs are sticking to it also, and I am dying—quite fast!"

"Poor thing," said the Mouse, "poor thing; I wish it was in my power to help you. It is really quite affecting; I am doomed to be the last survivor of all our cheerful little party!"

Then the Mouse sat with her head on her paw, in a mournful attitude, and meditated till morning.

"Here, Puss," said Sarah, the cook, "here is a Mouse for you. I thought I should catch you, Mrs. Cheese-nibbler!"

Then she opened the door, and out ran Mrs. Mouse in a terrible fright. She made straight for her hole, but a malicious coal-scuttle stood just before it, and would not get out of the way. So Puss hunted her about till she was quite tired of the sport, and then she ate her; remarking that "she was not over fat, but tender—very tender!"

"My dear," said Mrs. Brown, "I must get rid of that cat. The mischief she does is something frightful, and I really can't afford to keep such an expensive addition to the establishment. She has broken three jugs, seven china cups, a candlestick, three knives, and nineteen plates; besides devouring a ham, three chickens, a pigeon-pie, and a dish of cheese-cakes!"

"Bless my heart," said Dr. Brown, jumping up, "she costs more than a hundred mice. I'll give her a dose of Prussic acid, and you must do without a cat, my dear, and make Sarah set some traps!"

The fatal moment arrived—the doctor and the dose—and, in two minutes, poor Puss lay stretched lifeless on the grass-plat. Then the little Browns had a solemn funeral, and buried her under the gooseberry-bush.

"Heigh ho!" as the Mouse truly remarked—"Such is life!"

CPSIA information can be obtained
at www.ICGtesting.com
Printed in the USA
LVHW100447110522
718424LV00003B/275

9 783375 001254